GUARDIAN OF THE RED DESERT

THREADS OF THE LOST MYTH

JANYRE TROMP

ALSO BY JANYRE TROMP

—Threads of the Lost Myth Series—

History remembers. Myth echoes.

The truth lies between,

and every era weaves another fragment of the thread.

The Scorpion Thief

Guardian of the Red Desert (novella)

Burning the Raven Tree (coming September 2026)

The Oracle of the Silent City (coming March 2027)

—Standalone Titles—

Darkness Calls the Tiger

Shadows in the Mind's Eye

Lovely Life

Welcome back to the fight.

This time I know our side will win.

~Casblanca

1

Before roots remembered,

truth crossed the sky on a single breath,

riding the space between justice and mercy.

Where it touched earth, two forces stood.

One reached to lift truth, the other to bend it.

All the stories start here.

Fire tests us. Truth transforms us. And the shadows never die.

They only change their name.

~From *Origin of Myth*

Egypt
April 1943

A high whine snaps the man to attention. Captain Clifford "Hawkeye" Floyd blinks against the glare of the sun, his eyes flicking to search out the source of the anomaly. When you're flying at 220 miles per hour in the middle of the desert, any little problem can kill you fast as a knife through a hog carcass. But the prop spins at the tip of his faithful Warhawk's nose without a blip. Still, Cliff makes a visual sweep of the sky above him for a stray German 109 looking to pounce on the juicy, inexperienced pilots flying behind him. Blue sky stretches as far as he can see, the expanse only broken by the other Warhawks spread behind him, and the glare of sun on the rippled sand.

Wind screams through the tiny cracks in the canopy, and Cliff tightens his grip on the stick. Being back above the desert has him jumpier than a squirrel in a barrel. But there aren't any Jerries screaming out of the sun. At least not today.

He glances at his watch. They've been in the air for ninety minutes. Almost halfway to the next stop. After the short trip yesterday from Camp Huckstep to Fayid Airport in Cairo, his backside shouldn't be aching already. But it is. He looks at his instrument panel as he curves to a new heading, habit making him cautious as he confirms air speed and altitude. The instruments on his P-40 Warhawk flicker, jumping before settling into a comfortable normal. Except...

Swearing, he taps the compass and frowns as the pin grinds, popping and dragging.

His radio crackles, and an Ivy League voice crackles over the line, "Blue One, you see that on our—"

Cliff waits a minute, waiting for the cocky kid to resend. What had he seen? When the radio continues snapping in silence, Cliff clicks in. "Blue Three, come again?"

While he waits for Preston "Showboat" Ames to answer, Cliff twists, scanning the sky for bogeys. "You're flying a milk run," he mutters to himself. "An easy ferry to bring these planes to the China-Burma-India theater."

Except memory interrupts, jumping across his vision: the flicker of lights above the Sinai Canal, the whole sky stitched with tracers, red and green like the Fourth of July fireworks his little sister had once gotten hold of. Except it hadn't been a lark. His little P-40 shook while he dove, twisting, flying with wings perpendicular to the ground to avoid the anti-aircraft ordinance. Pulling back on the trigger, the recoil biting, jerking, louder than the corn thresher. Dust and cordite coating his teeth. Bandits swarming. The grinning face in the chaotic smoke. Couldn't hear nothing but the engine howling, the scream of the first Ames brother going down...

That's when Cliff realizes the past has bled right through to the present. The sky spreading across the horizon churns, orange and angry. Wind harnesses sand, pitching it into the sky, sparking the air with static electricity. He curses. A khamsin. The deadly dust storm must be what Showboat had spotted.

Cliff checks his maps and does a run-through of calculations in his mind. They're more than halfway to Wadi Halfa. If they keep on a steady heading, they might make it. He jots a note on the map and glances at the compass mounted on his instrument panel to confirm.

Except his needle shivers and comes to a complete standstill, pointing toward the wall of sand like a hunting dog. Of course his normally rugged plane would take this moment to completely malfunction. Cliff steers the plane in a lazy S-turn, rocking her a bit to see if the needle will wake up. But the pin stays steady in one place, no doubt jammed up with sand. P-40s are magnificently tough, except when it comes to sand. "Come on Sky King." When Cliff reaches to pull the knob on King's gyro to reset it, he notices the distinct knurled scratch pattern of a mis-torqued panel screw. No doubt a new mechanic. Cliff clenches his teeth against the flood of frustration.

Not his plane then. This is a human's doing. What else had the newbie gotten wrong?

He sucks in a breath and blows it out slowly. With more than thirty sorties under his belt, he's been in worse fixes before. At least that's what he tells himself as he peers over his port wing and picks out the telltale sparkle of the Nile. They could follow the river the rest of the way, but with the storm rolling in, the drift could push them miles off course. And, without a functioning compass, he wouldn't know a thing. He rubs at the ache pulsing in his forehead. He's been strapped with a herd of shavetails—pretty college boys who can quote Shakespeare but can't trim a Warhawk straight if their lives depended on it. And their lives may very well depend on it.

He can't help but think of Ginny's face falling last night when he told her he'd been volunteered for this run. She pleaded with him not to go. Her brown eyes filled with uncharacteristic tears. Resorted to hollering in a way she'd never done before. He should have known better than to laugh when she told him about some dream with ravens and falcons and a sky snake. A strange mix of his Uncle Paddy's creepy stories and the myths of Set and Horus spun by the locals. He'd only told her those stories so she'd snuggle into him. Ginny had merely scoffed then and parried his stories with the real-life horrors she'd seen on the streets in Chicago.

Which is why her reaction had been so strange. She knew he couldn't say no. When the brass asks you to go somewhere, you just nod and ask when to report. And he'd had other reasons to readily agree too. For one thing, he'd wanted to keep an eye on the younger Ames brother. Showboat didn't listen to anyone and would have run roughshod over any of the other, less experienced pilots. But then there were the things Cliff couldn't tell her. Things that sounded more like those Egyptian myths of sky serpents and gods of chaos than he'd like to admit.

Now he wishes he'd listened to her or at least hadn't brushed her off. But no. He puffed up his chest, acted like a hero, picked a fight. Blast his pride. She'd stood on the runway, arms dangling at her sides while prop wash tugged her dark curls out from under her white linen nurse's cap. He'd taken off, and he knew even then that he'd regret leaving her like that, maybe not today or even tomorrow. But he thought he'd have time. Turns out he might regret it sooner than he'd figured.

The pillar of sand rises higher, blotting out the sun. Cliff flicks on the control panel lights with a shaking hand. The wall of sand is still a ways off, but tiny bits of sand are already pinging against the plane.

"Blue One to Fayid." Despite his heart near beating out of his chest, Cliff's voice sounds bored as he calls the controller at the last airfield. Turn back or keep going? He needs advice, but there's no need to worry the pups. Showboat, especially. That kid routinely reacted to fear with a thick layer of overestimating his abilities. While the kid could use a tussle with one of Dad's angry hogs to set him straight, he doesn't deserve to die.

The radio snaps angrily, and Cliff curves with the arc of the river. If they lose sight of the river, the sand will swallow them whole, and their dried-out corpses might never be found. Sand collects in the creases of the plane's outer wall, the time ticking down before the storm hits, and he's out of time to make a decision.

"Bl—st—we?" Showboat's garbled voice rings with panic, and they haven't even reached the storm yet. Fortunately, the other planes are holding steady in tight formation even with knowledge of what's bearing down on them. If they can get above the storm before it hits fully, he can talk the others through navigation.

Cliff's engine skips, and he strokes the curved line of the console. "Come on, Sky King," he whispers. "You've always brought me home, even if you were filled with holes. Now's not the time to be finicky about a little dust." Whatever it cost, he'd get the other boys through, which means admitting he's not what they need right now. He learned that lesson the hard way.

"Blue Two?" Cliff calls up Argus. He's new, a college boy like the others, but Eugene "Argus" Owens grew up in the hills of Kentucky, and from the shadows in his eyes, the kid knows a thing or two. Cliff has no idea where Owens had picked up the nickname for the many-eyed sentinel from the old myths, but it fits: watchful, steady, loyal to a fault. The kind of man you want at your side as you face down Anubis. Not that Cliff is ready to meet the god of death just yet, and not that he believes in such things any more than he believes that Set, the god of chaos, is the one stirring the sands.

As if Cliff had summoned the gods, Sky King jolts underneath him, and the coolant temperature gauge surges toward the red arc. In front of him, a shimmer slicks over the prop wash—a sure sign the gauge reading is accurate. He eases off the throttle, giving in to the sluggish engine.

Black smoke bursts from the engine, sweeping off the cowl, engulfing the cockpit. Voices crackle over the radio, rolling over one another, cutting in and out, chaotic and panicking. Their planes may be flying smooth as the summer sky, but Cliff knows how terrifying it is to watch a friendly plane go down.

"Blue Two," Cliff shouts over the melee on the radio, "hightail it above this storm. My compass is shot, engine's redlining. Get your backside to Wadi Halfa. And tell Ginny she was right, and I'm sorry."

"Sir..." The line goes breathy.

"That's an order." And the last thing Cliff remembers is the laughing arc of otherworldly air slamming into Sky King's aluminum skin.

2

———

June 1943

Virginia Lenarsic normally thinks of herself as a patient woman. But when some blundering idiot pounds on her door a mere handful of minutes after she'd fallen, fully clothed, into bed, she nearly comes unglued.

She hasn't slept for...well, she doesn't know the last time she really slept. Since before Cliff disappeared two months ago, that much she's sure of.

The pounding comes again, and Ginny rolls off the bed onto all fours, hollering "What?" in the general vicinity of the door.

"Mail, ma'am." A woman's crisp British voice comes moments before a small paper-wrapped package onto the rough planks.

Mail? At—Ginny glances at the glowing hands of her watch—4 a.m.? Life at Camp Huckstep has never been normal, but this? She's suddenly wide awake, lunging through the door, over the package, and out onto the packed sand. A shadow swings around the corner, and Ginny, heedless of her disarrayed uniform, plunges onto the half-lit path.

At the sound of Ginny's clattering pursuit, the British woman, clad in the dark, loose clothing of a Bedouin tribe, turns. Her long braids swing over her shoulders, and her eyes go wide. She whirls and dives into the warren of tents and barracks. Ginny gives chase, but the woman knows what she's about. Even though Ginny is taller than the woman by a full head, she's barely keeping up as she slogs through the half-kept sandy paths. And when an enormous black dog lunges in front of Ginny, the other woman disappears like a puff of smoke behind the sprawling thousand-bed hospital. Then a shrill whistle sounds and the dog lopes off after what must be his master. Ginny grouses at all the dumb luck.

What kind of mail could a Bedouin woman possibly have for her? But then there was that voice—refined, distinctly British. An odd combination.

Ginny shakes her head. Her father's mission in inner-city Chicago had taught her better than to size up a person based on what they looked like. She's seen society ladies step around broken children and a beggar give the same child his last crust. But why would someone with that voice dress in Bedouin robes? Who is she? And what was she doing so far from normal trade routes and with mail for a random combat nurse, no less?

Sighing, Ginny trudges back to her tent, retrieves the bundle from the ground, and drops it onto the single desk tucked between the bunks she shares with her roommate Carlotta, and the occasional other nurse headed from here to wherever. She knows she won't sleep now before her shift rolls around again.

Her roommate has the night shift and will be back in a few hours, wondering what Ginny is doing, still up and still unpacked for home. But she can't leave now, can she?

She twirls the little engagement ring on her finger. When Cliff had gone missing, the Army had given her a few days' leave to grieve, and she'd nearly gone crazy with too much time to think. And that isn't a euphemism. She'd found herself standing on a hotel fire escape ten stories up, wondering if the pain would stop if she jumped. The thought skittering through her brain made her recoil from the edge, wondering where the urge had come from. That was the second time she heard the laughter.

Not like you hear in the next room or across the table. It's crazy. *She* is crazy. But she could swear the sound came from the other side of the veil of time, from another world. She doesn't know how to explain it better than that. Like she's in a dream, maybe, except achingly awake.

Ginny sits, staring at the package, leg jiggling with...she doesn't even know what. Fear? Anticipation? Which is silly. She doesn't even know if it's for her.

She lets out a little laugh and flips the bundle over. There's no name. No address. No sign of who it is for or where it came from. She drops her hands into her lap. It's probably something from one of Carlotta's admirers.

And yet, Ginny can't make herself stand and go back to bed. She taps a finger on the package, and it thumps with the happy solidity of a book. Any man hoping to woo Carlotta would not be sending a book, which means it's probably for Ginny, right?

Under the circumstances, Carlotta will forgive her for opening the package if it wasn't meant for Ginny. Decision made, Ginny carefully cracks open the package's brown paper and stops cold.

A raven is stamped clear as day on the back.

Cliff used to tell her his Uncle Paddy's stories. The tales of the Tuatha Dé Danaan, the powerful Celtic race, and she laughed that the Tuatha had become the Little People, destined to be shoved underground and mostly ignored. Dad told her similar stories passed down from his family of the spirits and dwarves who might be benevolent one day and brutal the next. She'd been fascinated by all the crossover in stories, almost like they all started from one story and splintered into odd pieces at some point.

But then Cliff told her of the Morrígan—the warrior woman who would shift into the form of a powerful raven in full battle ornament. "She was brilliant," Cliff had said, "and brutal when she had to be. Kind of like the stories of the Egyptian goddess Aset...and someone else I know." He'd nudged her shoulder.

But Ginny isn't as strong as he'd thought. Every stone-cold decision she has made about who will have a chance with a doctor and who will die has carved out her soul until, every night, she wakes to the barking caw of the Morrígan's voice.

Then the laughter sprouted up, then the dream of a falcon shouting down the raven's voice as a serpent slipped out of the sky to devour the world. And it all started the night before Cliff left, like some premonition.

No wonder she's a wreck.

She yanks open the rest of the paper and frowns. Inside the package are two books: one a small pocket-sized notebook stamped with "U.S. Army Air Force Pilot Flight Log," and the other a leather-bound journal. Ginny picks up the flight log. The edges of the hardcover are scuffed thin, and the pages bear the distinct char of fire. Ginny's fingers shake as she flips the book open.

An engineer's precise letters shoulder their way across the page: *Clifford "Hawkeye" Floyd.*

Pressure builds inside Ginny's head, the banshee scream of the khamsin building behind her ears, until she drops the book and bolts away from the little desk, sending the wooden chair clattering against the floor.

"You okay?" Carlotta's voice brims with uncontained concern.

Ginny wheels, frantically scraping together her composure. How long had her roommate been standing there? What had she seen? High command won't allow her to re-up her commitment if they think she belongs in an asylum. "Yes, of course. Just thought I saw a scorpion."

Carlotta shivers. "I hate those things." She shimmies out of her uniform and then drops onto her bed. "I swear you get less sleep than I do these days."

Ginny gives her a weak smile. "And yet, I have no social calendar."

"Oh, honey." Carlotta wraps an arm around her friend. "You say the word and we'll fix that for you."

Pushing to her feet, Ginny tucks the books into her footlocker, resisting the urge to lock it. She and Carlotta had been to hades together and trusted one another with their lives. Carlotta wouldn't snoop. "I'm just not ready yet."

"Of course not. Cliff was a good man."

Ginny cringes at Carlotta's use of the past tense. Cliff's plane hasn't been found, yet she knows he has to be dead. "I still turn to tell him things." She folds the bottom of her crumpled uniform skirt and then straightens it again, smoothing it flat like that might straighten out her life. "We were going to change the world, you know? He was going to come to Chicago, start a farmer's market to sell his friend's produce to the folks at Dad's mission. Farm-fresh food and medical care." A harsh laugh escapes her lips. "It sounds so stupid when I say it out loud."

"Not at all." Carlotta's broad Boston accent smashes the words all together. "It was a lovely idea. And far better than my plan to just escape the craziness of the Abrams household and go someplace where no one hollers at me for no reason."

"So you joined the army?" Ginny laughs at the irony.

"Well." Carlotta shrugs, her dark eyes sparkling. "For one they're far more handsome. And yes, they holler. But they've always got a reason."

"Speaking of . . ." Ginny glances at her watch.

"You best get going, kid." Carlotta shoos her roommate out the door, and Ginny hugs her friend.

"I don't know what I'd do without you."

"Right back atcha. Now get out of here so I can sleep."

Ginny exits the tent and trudges through a fresh layer of sand that had blown over the paths in the last hour. Part of her wonders if the encounter with the Bedouin woman had been real, but she has no way to track her. Best to be like her dad—be grateful for the blessings that drop in your lap and not wait for the other shoe to smash into your noggin.

⚲

Two days later, Ginny finally has half a second alone in the tent to pull out the bundle. This time, it's midnight, and she's snuggled into her bunk. Even though the temperature has finally dropped below ninety, sweat drips down her back, gathering in unseemly pools. Back home in Chicago, they'd complain about eighty degrees, and Lake Michigan was always a short ride away. It all seemed so naive now. Naive and idyllic despite the drudgery of her daily life and the hardship she'd seen.

She clicks on her flashlight and wedges it into the bunk above her. Sucking in a breath, she sets the books on her lap. Where does she start? A leather cord dangles from the flight log like a bookmark. So

Ginny flips to the marked page. Nestled on top of Cliff's neat, square writing is a strange red pendant attached to the cord.

She flips the oval stone over. It's almost human in form—a looped head, arms pressed against the prostrate body, a knot on its chest. The knot is what reminds her. She's seen this symbol before. With Cliff. At the museum in Cairo. Something to do with a goddess who'd raised her husband from the dead?

She shuts her eyes, thinking of the artifacts spilling from cases. Cliff's voice reading the faded little cards. The mango ice he'd purchased from a street vendor, the rose he'd pricked his finger on before removing all the thorns and tucking it into her hair. Ginny sucks in a shuddering breath. He'd been the first man to treat her with the respect her father treats her mother. The first man she'd thought she could spend forever with.

Maybe these pages will tell her what happened. Her palm warms against the necklace. Does she want to know? She'd held on to the fraying thread of hope for weeks. Did she want it snapped?

She knows Cliff hadn't been negligent like some of the other flyboys said. He was too careful, too determined to prove himself to do something stupid.

Ginny ties the amulet around her neck. Surely knowing is better than this limbo. She bends to read the entry from the flight log.

> Date: 14 April 1943
> Aircraft: P-40F #41-20317 "Sky King"
> Mission: Ferry (Cairo West to Wadi Halfa)
> Sortie Time: 0925-1320 (3 hrs 55 min)
> Remarks: Compass unreliable. Khamsin rolled in—visibility nil. Temp gauge redlined, engine rough. Blue Two in trail. Solo forced landing west of the Nile.

Letting her finger track down the page, Ginny imagines Cliff in the cockpit, huddled over the journal, calmly filling in the details while he waits for Argus to call in reinforcements.

And the cavalry had been called, had gone out, but then found nothing but a swath of unbroken sand and a few rocks where the other pilots had seen Cliff go down. Of course there had been a sandstorm, and with the pilots being green as spring grass, maybe they got it wrong.

Ginny stiffens. But if no one found his plane, where had the log come from? Is this an elaborate hoax? She can't imagine why someone would create a fake journal, but it is possible. Isn't it?

She drops the flight log and picks up the other book—an army-issue green memo book. The white pages are dark with grime, the corners curl in on themselves like they might be hiding from whatever words are scrawled across the pages.

Sucking in a breath, Ginny opens it and smiles at the sketches sprawling across the first pages. A dog, Ginny herself in profile, the proud Sphynx. Probably from the last few days they had together, well before Cliff had been voluntold to ferry the planes to the CBI. This, at least, is assuredly one of Cliff's notebooks. Had someone stolen it from his locker before the Army sent his effects home?

She flips past entries until she sees the date he'd been swallowed by the desert, and she starts to read.

My dearest Virginia,

As I am sure you have heard by now, I had engine trouble and was forced down near Luxor, as far as I can reckon. Argus is a good man and keeps his head about him. Doesn't surprise me. He was solid in training too. He may look like one of those uppity college boys always bothering you, but he got to telling me about life in Kentucky with his sisters and folks. Learning is important to them, but Eugene's been hunting since he was knee high to a tadpole. He is sure to have gotten a good enough reading on where I am, and he'll be sending help soon. As long as Showboat doesn't give him too much trouble. That kid is pain from the word go.

But they may not be able to get to me until the storm passes, which means I have time to sit and write. Something you know is always in short supply.

At the moment, I am safe enough inside my cockpit. The wind is beating against the windows, but only a tiny string of sand has found its way through. I can near hear you saying, "I told you so," but you also know I couldn't say no. I hate that I'll be the source of your fretting. I do wish you were here...or rather, I wish I was there with you. I could use an aspirin and cold water.

And since you'll likely not read this until I'm home safely, I could use your stitching abilities. The gash on my head is going to heal all sideways and give me a rather pirate look. It'll be something for the college boys to be in awe of, I suppose. Either that or something for them to point at and say that I'm not worthy to fly.

Nothing I haven't heard before. Course none of them are aces, and none of them have you. I'll close my eyes now and dream of your sweet voice regaling me with the antics of your brother. I'm sure he'll grow up to be a lawyer, but someday I'll meet Marcus and teach him how to race a car for real.

Ginny clenches her teeth against the tears. She will not give in. Will not imagine her brainiac, squirrelly brother whooping with Cliff through the cornfields of Iowa. She will not imagine her laughter, the cool Chicago breeze tousling Cliff's hair as he reads to the kids at the mission like he had with his kid sister. Ginny bites the inside of her cheek and flips past the words, hunting for more of Cliff's rough sketches.

The next page is a drawing of the Eye of Horus, then the shape of the pendant she's wearing with the name Aset penned below it. Next to her name, he'd written "protection" and underlined it. Ginny can practically hear him promising that he'd protect her. While he was the last person to believe in the hocus-pocus of the ancient myths, he was also the first person to make sure Ginny felt safe without making her feel manipulated in the process.

Ginny turns the page and frowns. There, a strange creature stares at her from the corner of its eye. An anteater's nose curves slightly down, and the forked tail flickers near its tall ears. The lines are drawn hard as if Cliff had gone over them repeatedly, frantically. She rubs a thumb over the gouges in the paper. Why would he be so—

Her flashlight flickers then snaps out.

Swearing under her breath, Ginny bangs the light on her palm. But the thing refuses to work. In the distance, a dog bays at the moon.

Ginny bunches her sheet against her chest. The only light comes from the glowing hand of her watch, which points to the two. She has to be up for her shift in just a few hours. She lies down even though she knows she won't sleep much and tucks the books under her pillow. Maybe, just maybe, she won't have nightmares tonight.

3

____

I hope I've done the right thing. Last night, my master once again thundered at me. Shouting that I am chaos when I am meant to be quiet and protection. But how can I be those things when he does what he does?

I am afraid that by giving the woman the books, I will make things worse. But the American flyer's words haunt me: "How can you do nothing when to be quiet means to be complicit? How can you be quiet when you know there is danger under the surface only a few can see?"

Yet violence is sometimes necessary, is it not? Otherwise the serpent would swallow the world. So I chase this course into the very mouth of the cold death of Duat.

Perhaps my descendants will forgive me. Perhaps they will see my fight for what it is—supporting the chaos that ends true evil.

But I fear it will not be enough. That this cycle of betrayal will never end. I call the red sand and it swirls, hiding my frail human form and pulling me into my father's night boat. May the *mesektet* fly true tonight.

4

____

Ginny jerks awake to the jolting bugle call of the reveille and bangs her head on the bunk above her. She stifles a curse and rubs her smarting forehead until the sting dulls enough that she can swing her legs off the bed. She had slept, cocooned in uninterrupted sleep, but she needed a week's worth more.

Carlotta pops into the tent, giggling and dragging a square-jawed man behind her. At the squeak of bedsprings, Carlotta swings around, her big, innocent eyes going even wider. "You're still here?"

Ginny waves off her roommate's mix of concern and consternation and steps behind a little screen to throw on her nurse's uniform. She smooths out the wrinkles then tugs her mass of hair into a low bun and struggles to pin her cap on top. She bites back tears of frustration at the stupid Army regulations requiring her to keep her hair off her collar. Maybe tomorrow she'll cut it all off. She'd been growing her hair out for the wedding. But now? What's the point? Ginny tucks the pendant under her collar and shoves her feet into her shoes.

In the time it takes for the El to screech along its elevated rails and grind to a stop, she's slipping past her roommate's new paramour and trotting up the path to the hospital. It's only when she swings past one of the orderlies folding linens that she remembers the books, the amulet, and her miraculously blank sleep. But she can only contemplate the connection between books and sleep for a moment before the charge nurse starts barking orders.

A fresh batch of broken boys has arrived, and each of them is in dire need of pain meds, a bed, and a friendly face. A deep shout in the distance makes Ginny stumble, barely catching herself as the memory of the first time she'd met Cliff slams into her mind. His deep voice demanding help. Ginny started to give him what for until she saw the boy in his arms. She'd found out later that the boy had burned his hand trying to steal Cliff's breakfast.

Cliff had made sure the boy was treated and then hired him to do semi-useless running about just so the boy had food to eat. Cliff had paid the boy out of his own money and then hired his little sister too. Not that he could afford it. He was notoriously in debt with the other grunts, but no one seemed to overly mind. When Cliff disappeared, Ginny had checked around for the child, but he'd disappeared like smoke—like Cliff himself had.

♀

Eight hours later, Ginny's head is about to explode, and her stomach isn't happy with her either, not to mention her aching feet. Her breakfast of dry toast and coffee had been far too long ago. But there's been one patient after another needing immediate help.

Thank goodness the flood has finally turned to a trickle. After this patient, she'll see about a little food and some aspirin. Her charges deserve a nurse who isn't about to fall over.

Ginny lifts another chart for another man with another wound. This one...she skims the technical jargon...has a burn on his face and neck. "Well." She turns and tries not to recoil at the poor man's melted cheek and nose. "Let's get some antibiotics and fresh bandages, shall we? How's your pain?" She forces herself to look into his clouded eyes and wait, unflinching.

The man—little more than a boy—slowly focuses on her, his tough, I-feel-no-pain mask pulling into a frown. "Ginny?"

Bile leaps from Ginny's gut as she searches his face, his eyes. Who? She stares at the paperwork. Desperate, terrified to discover which of her friends this is, her brain flails to focus, to make out the words. Finally, a name floats up from the tangle of words—Eugene Owens. "Argus?"

She wraps a hand around the footrail and blinks away the sparks of darkness filling her vision until she can focus on his haunted puppy-dog eyes. "Do you need more pain medication?" Her voice cracks, and she silently scolds herself for the display of emotion.

He starts to shake his head no but seizes with pain.

That is answer enough for her. She turns, unlocks the cabinet, pulls out the sulfa powder, a morphine bottle, and a fresh syringe, and measures a quarter-grain of morphine.

"You don't need to be a hero in here. Keeping your pain under control will help you sleep, and that will help you heal." She swabs the rubber port on the IV and slowly feathers in the medicine. Her attention sweeps between the second hand on her watch and the rise and fall of his chest.

"I'm not going to—" Argus swallows and swings his eyes around the room in panic. "They'll follow me here too."

Ginny leans over him to dust his wounds with the sulfa powder. "Who will follow you?"

His hand latches onto her wrist. She tries to wrench back, but he's got a solid grip on her, and his expression has gone deadly. "Are you one of them?"

"Argus," she says as calmly as her tightened vocal cords will allow. "You know me. I don't even know who 'they' are. You're safe here. With the antibiotics and care here, you'll be just fine. I'll make sure of it."

She means it. She's seen thousands of men recover from similar burns and be shipped back home. But Argus shakes his head and reaches across his body to touch the pendant that has fallen free of her uniform. It swings on its strap, and he watches it, mesmerized. "Who gave it to you?"

She opens her mouth to answer *Cliff,* but she lays her hand over the warm stone, unsure who the woman was or if the pendant was the woman's or Cliff's. She'd never seen it on Cliff before. "Honestly?" Her laugh is breathy, insubstantial. "Some woman. I assume she's one of the wives of the traders. I don't know her name."

"He knew," Argus says. "He knew, and I promised Cliff I'd look after you. But I'm afraid—" Argus blinks and releases her wrist. He settles his hands across his chest like he's preparing to lie down in a coffin. The thought sends a shiver down her spine.

"Who knew? And what do you mean you promised Cliff to look after me?" When he doesn't answer, Ginny eases into the hard chair at his bedside.

"Just be careful." His eyes flutter open. "There are...things...people, I guess, that aren't what they seem."

"Are you in some kind of trouble?"

"Don't lose that pendant."

"Why?"

"Just don't say anything to anyone about any of this."

"What are you talking about?"

"If you don't know, they can't come after you like they did us."

"Us? Who is us?"

But Argus turns his head away and clenches his eyes shut. Ginny thinks about Cliff's journal. He's only mentioned two men. Argus and—

"Does this have something to do with Showboat?"

Argus doesn't answer, but his nose flares the tiniest bit. Enough for Ginny to know she's on to something.

"What's going on, Argus? What does Showboat have to do with whoever they are?"

But there's no reaction now.

Ginny quickly finishes bandaging the burns, then leans back. "You can't refuse to talk to me forever." Although that's not entirely true. He may not return to the battlefield, but he's stable enough that they'll ship him home sooner rather than later. And Argus was the last person to see Cliff alive.

Another soldier cries out for help, and she pivots toward him. "I'll be there in just a minute." The veneer of polite is thin. Ginny's normally unflappable demeanor has come undone, flapping wildly in an onrushing storm.

"Argus?"

But he is silent, and the soldier at the end of the ward cries again. Turning back to the pilot, Ginny leans over and whispers, "I'll be back tomorrow. You rest now."

GINNY NEVER DOES GET MORE to eat during her shift, and so, by the time she stumbles from the hospital, she's in no mood for soldiers trying to flirt or for questionable mashed potatoes. She wishes her dinner options were better. She might sell her soul for a steak from Henrici's or even a decent burger.

As it is, she settles for the Army's three food groups—Spam, beans, and hash—all thrown into a stew. Thankfully, some saint has slipped in fresh tomatoes and onions from the market, which makes the goo almost edible. And one of the cooks smuggled her a mango as a thanks for stitching up his arm without questioning why he'd gotten into a knife fight. It tastes like sunshine and quiet fields and is one of the few things that can clear the gritty sand out of her mouth.

In the time she's been in Egypt, Ginny's had to take in her uniform more than a few times. Mom will absolutely panic with how much weight her daughter has lost. Cliff couldn't care less about how she filled out her uniform, but even he had groused about how little she ate. What would he think now?

Just as Ginny sips the last of her coffee, Carlotta drops into the seat across from her. "I'm going to marry that man."

Grinning at her roommate's flushed cheeks, Ginny reaches across the table and straightens Carlotta's collar. Who is she to caution her friend about the flyboys and their penchant to fly away? All the nurses knew the risks. Still...

"You spent the whole day with him?"

"Of course not. He's from London. Has the best accent, but you know his daddy isn't going to like a spitfire Bostonian in his family. That boy will have to do more than make moon eyes at me."

Carlotta takes a bite of the stew, careful not to disturb her bright red lipstick, and grimaces. "Maybe I can talk him into taking me to Shepheard's Hotel for a decent dinner. I'm going to waste away on this gruel.

Or maybe they'll let me into the kitchen. Surely there's something better than Spam soup." She takes another sip, then spouts a rip of Italian that Ginny can't make heads or tails of despite having worked with more than a few immigrants in Chicago.

"At least the bread's good." Ginny nods at the golden disc on Carlotta's plate.

"Ach. These"—Carlotta pokes at the flatbread—"aren't bad. But you should taste my grandmother's focaccia."

Ginny straightens the silverware next to her empty bowl. Home. Maybe she should just catch the next transport to the States and be done with this place. And yet, she can't get Argus's mangled face out of her mind. That he is afraid is clear. He hadn't reacted well to her mention of Showboat, but there seemed to be more...and what would Showboat have to do with a Bedouin woman who speaks perfect King's English?

"You okay?" Carlotta watches her friend, brow wrinkled with concern.

Of anyone left in Camp Huckstep, Carlotta is the one person who can read Ginny's normally stoic face. But Argus had warned her not to say anything to anyone, had suggested he'd been targeted, that she would be next if anyone found out she had more information.

"I—" Ginny slides her hands into her lap. No, she can't drag her friend into any of this. "I'm just hot...and tired...and Argus was in my ward today."

Carlotta sighs and reaches a hand across the table. "I am so sorry, honey." Carlotta's hands are remarkably smooth despite the dry air and constant handwashing.

Ginny's look like a day laborer's—as cracked and dried as she feels.

"I'm going to just try to get some sleep."

Carlotta pats Ginny's fingers and then leans back. "I'll check in on him during my shift and see you in the morning."

Ginny manages a nod, cleans up her dirty dishes, and trudges through the door. Outside the din of the mess hall is replaced with the odd, distant chatter of men. The pop-pop-pop of the .30 caliber carbines marches in rhythm with her feet. She's inordinately thankful she's not out in the sunbaked range at this time of day. She swats at a fly and ducks around the corner, skirting the officer's headquarters in favor of the shade of the hospital. In the distance, a jackal complains, and Ginny agrees.

A shadow flickers over her head, and she ducks instinctively. When she straightens, she scans the sky and, there, a bird sits on the roof across the way, studying her with one dark eye. He's backlit by the sun, and she can't make out much. A falcon? He cries at her, shaking his wings out. She knows next to nothing about birds, but it feels like a warning. And combined with Argus's strange behavior, she decides to bank into the sunlight toward the main thoroughfare through camp.

She feels ridiculous scurrying away from a bird. But then she hears the scuffle of feet behind her, and she comes up short, turning before her brain can tell her not to. In the shadows, a man watches her, not more than two steps away. His eyes are so wide she wonders if he even has lids. And the pupils—are they slitted like a snake's? She backs up a pace and then another, one hand closing over the chill of the pendant and the other over Cliff's old combat knife. The man's tongue flicks across his thin lips. If she didn't know better, she'd swear the pink tip is split into a fork. How is that possible? Somewhere a voice screams in her head to run. But she's unable to pull herself away from the depths of his dark eye sockets.

"Stop sticking your nose where it should not be," he hisses. He steps toward her and Ginny snaps awake. She flees into the road lined with barracks and men, not stopping until she's in the scant protection of her tent.

Inside, she snags the books from under her mattress and scampers behind the screen, dragging the chair with her. She knows enough to get any height advantage she can. She'd picked that tidbit up from the kids at the shelter back home. As she stands on the chair clutching a combat knife Cliff insisted she carry, she knows how abominably vulnerable she is.

Laughter lifts from the far side of the camp—high and unhinged. She nearly drops the knife at the familiar echo. She knows without seeing that it belongs to the snake man. That she hadn't imagined the voice, the eyes. Something is out there hunting her.

♀

Darkness still swaths the room when Ginny starts. At some point, she fell awake. She's leaning against the wall. Why is she—and then she remembers, scrambling to find the knife, then clambering to her feet.

"Ginny?" Carlotta's whispering voice makes Ginny burst into tears, and she flings herself around the screen into her startled roommate's arms.

"What's wrong?" Carlotta makes a brave attempt to stand under her much taller friend's assault, but she stumbles back a few steps before regaining her balance.

Ginny gives a garbled recitation of of what happened with the man, her flight back to the tent, and even though she can't see her friend's raised perfectly shaped eyebrows, Ginny knows she sounds like she's off her rocker. Really, a snake man? Still, Carlotta shushes her friend and leads her to the bunk where they collapse side by side. Somehow Carlotta manages to corral her much taller friend against her shoulder. The action makes Ginny think of her mother and Chicago and none of this can be real, can it?

"I don't know." Ginny smooths her hair back into the bun on top of her head. "It's probably because I'm exhausted and worried about Argus and..."

Carlotta hasn't said anything, but the stiffening of her shoulders and the sigh escaping her lips make Ginny leap to her feet. Anything to get away from whatever is happening. "Why are you back so early?"

"Why don't you sit back down?" Carlotta pats the bed, but Ginny spins and paces.

"No one ever wants me to sit unless there's something bad to say. What happened?"

Carlotta blinks back tears and pulls a note from her pocket, extending it to Ginny. "I'm so sorry. Argus...he didn't make it."

A bomb goes off inside Ginny. She cannot hear, cannot feel, cannot see. "He was fine. He..." But then she remembers the fear in his eyes, his command to not tell anyone, to be careful. Maybe the snake man is real after all.

"He had some weird infection." Carlotta shrugs.

"He showed no signs of—"

"I saw him, Ginny. He's better off. It was..." Carlotta's eyes flutter, flashing with anger and anguish before forcing a smile back on her face. There's nothing more to say.

After a full thirty minutes of Ginny assuring Carlotta that she's fine, Carlotta swishes out the door.

"Wait." Ginny jumps from the bunk, holding whatever missive Argus had for her. "Can I borrow your flashlight?"

But Carlotta is already gone. Ginny stands, listening to the creaking of the tent ropes around her. Carlotta keeps her flashlight in her foot-locker and won't mind if Ginny borrows it, especially under the circumstances.

Carlotta's footlocker is a study in chaos. How the woman finds anything is beyond Ginny, but her friend always seems to know exactly where everything is—from her uniform shoes to a hairpin. And there, twisted in a gauzy linen shirt, is the flashlight.

Ginny opens the letter from Argus. The words are barely legible and certainly not the penmanship of any of the nurses. Had he managed to write it himself? She turns the page over, looking for the initials of someone who had acted as scribe. But there is nothing there.

Sighing, Ginny squints at the mass of jumbled letters.

Don't talk to anyone here. I'm sorry I lied.
Pretty sure Showboat tampered with Cliff's plane. I gave wrong information to protect Cliff. I couldn't get out to tell anyone the right coordinates because SB said I was feeding intel to some reporter. When they found a bent torque wrench in my kit, SB claimed I'd botched Cliff's maintenance check on purpose because Cliff knew about the reporter. I ended up in the brig. I swear, when they dragged me in, there was a man watching—his eyes were too dark, too wide, like he wasn't human. Maybe you can find out what really happened. Cliff was really northwest of Luxor. 25°45'N, . . .

The series of numbers slant down, running, blurring, until finally, they fall off the page in a snaking streak. Ginny shoots to her feet. Are these what she thinks they are? But Argus had been afraid to give anyone at Camp Huckstep the coordinates, and not even twelve hours after she'd talked to a completely coherent Argus, he was dead. The paper crinkles a warning in Ginny's hand.

"Cliff," she whispers, "what did you get yourself into?"

5

With nowhere else to go, Ginny settles back behind the folding screen, this time with her pillow and Carlotta's flashlight. She opens Cliff's journal and flips to the first entries after the drawings—the ones she'd skipped.

> *Tonight I plan to take Nurse Virginia Lenarsic—Ginny, she said to call her—to Cairo. Me. A man with no fancy degree or pedigree name. Back home, none of that would matter. The Floyd name is good as any other.*
>
> *But out here, anyone who's anyone has a college degree and their names listed on buildings. And if they don't have that, they at least have parents who have names that make people stop and pay attention. Ginny didn't choose any of them. She agreed to come with me. I still can't believe it.*

"Oh, Cliff." Ginny leans back into the pillow on her rock-hard bunk. "Always trying to prove yourself got you into more trouble."

. . .

THE SECOND TIME she'd seen him, he came into the hospital with a slice above his eyebrow and a split lip. He had obviously been in a scrap, but was calm, saying "yes, ma'am...no, ma'am," and barely looking at her. She thought at first it was shame, but her mess hall friend Frankie came traipsing in behind Cliff, begging her to take good care of the fool pilot. After all, he, Frankie, was the reason Cliff had ended up in the hospital.

The fool had stepped between a raging pilot and the tiny tech corporal, saying, "Chow isn't no reason to get upset. Least we have food to eat." The pilot took exception to Cliff's interference and making him look like a jerk. "The fool is all heart. But all that flaming red hair burned up some of his brain cells. But," and here Frankie grinned, "Cliff has kept up his hand-to-hand combat skills, and the other idiot flyboy let his lapse."

Said idiot pilot, Worthington Ames, had tried to jump Cliff and learned his lesson. He came in a minute later, wailing like a tenement radiator in January and hollering at anything that wasn't serving him the moment he thought he deserved something. Pretty typical of the normal flyboy.

When Worthington hollered at Ginny, she was sure Cliff was going to cold-cock Worthington again then and there. She asked him not to... and he hadn't. Of course he laughed when Ginny, who outranked the jerk, dressed him down in fine fashion.

When she turned back to Cliff with "see?" clearly communicated in her raised eyebrows, Frankie made moon eyes at her and said he loved a woman who could take care of herself. And Cliff? Well, he just gave her a smirking half smile and a thumbs up.

When she found out he wasn't just a flyboy but a fighter pilot, she'd been curious. How come a cocky pilot was so gentle and respectful to a nobody like her? Most of the fighter pilots chased skirts and bragged about dropping enemies into the drink all day, whether it was true or not.

Curious, she checked around and found out he was a bona fide ace, that he tended to use his fists rather than his mouth to settle arguments, and ended up giving away more than he earned. But he also had a little sister he was fiercely protective of, and—the part that made everything make sense—a hog farm back home with a mama who'd flay him alive if he so much as wolf-called a woman. The latter two bits she'd heard from Frankie.

Most of the other flyboys learned real quick to take Cliff seriously. But Worthington Ames's high-ranking daddy bailed him out more times than sand got in Ginny's shoes. As a result, Worthington had become an entitled jerk. Something his little brother had picked right up and carried on too.

Ginny bites her lip, thinking of Argus's reaction to Showboat's name. And the mention of Showboat's accusations. At the very least, the younger Ames brother had spiked Argus's career. But is Showboat guilty of more than just jealousy? She has no proof of anything other than Argus's word. And she knows that won't be enough. Not with who Showboat's daddy is and not with what had happened to Worthington.

Ginny bites her lip and goes back to reading.

My little sister is a bit of a hellion, but only because folks don't see how amazing she is, and they try to stuff her in a pretty little box. Ginny reminds me a little of Roberta Jane. All fiery and smart and stubborn. But heaven knows Ginny is as gorgeous as Helen of Troy. And probably as much trouble.

Most of the flyboys aren't at all like Moe back home. I learned real quick that, unlike my best friend, who'd give a man the shirt off his back, these kind don't take kindly to farm boys and would "accidentally" bump my tools during a flight check or crowd my wings to rattle me. But they found out I don't flinch, I don't get lost, and I don't freeze when a trainer drops me in a stall and spin.

They hated me before, but when they realized I was stepping out with Ginny, you'd think I'd set the world on fire.

Ginny grins. What would they have done if they realized she'd contrived to get him to ask her out? She'd stood outside the mess hall for forever—talking to Carlotta and then pretending to read a book—waiting for him to emerge from dinner. When he finally appeared, he saw her, smiled, then said, "Out of all the mess halls in the world, she walks into mine."

Like she set the stars in the sky.

And then he laughed, the heavens opening with their reckless abandon. Truly a Sky King, just as his nose portrayed. She fell in next to Cliff, telling him she missed seeing him for check-ups on the stitches, practically begging him to ask her out. Her father would have nudged her shoulder in encouragement, glad she'd spoken up for herself. On the other hand, her mother would have been horrified—not that her daughter was interested in the smart, handsome farmer but that she'd made her interest so glaringly plain.

Ginny heard the way the others talked about him, saw how they treated him. He'd been an outsider.

She still can't understand why. From the moment she stitched him up, she was fascinated with the intensely quiet pilot. He wasn't handsome in a chiseled Adonis way. But those deep blue eyes had reminded her of Lake Michigan in the summer, and his auburn locks, rebelliously cut longer than regulation, made her want to run her fingers through them just to see if she could make him quirk a smile.

Her fingers slide over the pendant she'd found in the book. She blinks back tears.

Ginny skims the next few pages of Cliff's wandering thoughts, his sketches, his heart-wrenching goodbye when he shipped off to Italy, and then his elated return. And then:

I stopped in at Groppi's Café this morning. I'd promised Nikos to show him Mom's famous Irish apple cake. Of course we had to modify the recipe. Not many apples in Cairo, but Nikos brought quince, which was a stroke of genius—something we could easily find but with the tartness rivaling Granny Smiths from back home.

We were just drizzling crème anglaise over the top when Showboat Ames traipsed in, smoking like a late freight train. He growled at the server that stepped up to help, seeming to not have learned his manners from his older brother, and then plopped down across from a man in a western suit with a notepad in front of him. I had half a mind to have a conversation with the younger brother when the server tucked something into his pocket and turned with a wicked smile on his lined face.

The server had lifted a bauble from the pilot. Like Ginny, he'd exacted his own revenge and didn't need my interference.

I let my attention drift back to the shadowy corner. My hands clenched around the ladle Nikos had handed me. Alarm bells blared in my head. Showboat was shaking like he was nervous. The man across from him sat, ramrod straight. Like a soldier...but dressed all wrong and with that notepad...

I asked Nikos if he was some kind of reporter and Nikos grunted. "He'd like everyone to think so."

When I asked what he meant, Nikos grabbed the ladle, poured the custard over the cake, and handed me a fork. "If Peter Monkaster is an American newspaper reporter, my name is Bob, and I'm from Chicago."

Clicking off the flashlight to preserve the battery, Ginny curls her fingers around the journal. If this Monkaster gentleman isn't a reporter, who is he? And what was Showboat doing talking to him?

Showboat had a chip on his shoulder from the moment he walked into the barracks and finding Cliff getting another commendation. The one he'd gotten for trying to save his older brother's hide.

Showboat didn't seem to care that after the incident in the mess hall, Worthington had twice bailed on his wingman to try to tag an easy kill. If he had been any other flyer, he would have been disciplined after the mess hall and grounded after he exposed his wingman. But Lt. Col. Albert Ames had pulled strings for his son. So he was in the air again as Cliff's wingman. Unfortunately, Worthington hadn't learned his lesson. The minute he split off, he drew the attention of a 109 diving out of the cloud cover. Worthington got his kill, but Cliff wasn't been able to swing back around in time to save him.

Showboat swore he'd make Cliff pay, tried to draw him into a fight. Cliff understood the grief and ducked his clumsy swings, which only made Showboat more angry, and he trashed the conference room. Showboat ended up on KP duty under Frankie. Just like his big brother. Cliff gave him space to hopefully cool down and learn his lesson...something any other flyer would be doing in the brig.

Ginny bites her lip, afraid of whatever is coming. She remembers when Cliff came home from that trip to Cairo. He had a slice of the cake and, even though he was fuming mad, he refused to talk to her. Right or wrong, he'd tried to protect her to the end.

But Ginny was stronger stuff than Cliff knew, and if he was concerned, someone had to do something, right? She wraps her hand around the pendant and clicks the flashlight back on.

Peter Monkaster slid an envelope across the table, and Showboat stood, leaving a bag behind.

Monkater sucked in on his cigarette, the end glowing red, as he watched Showboat scuttle away like a beetle. When he blew out, the smoke swirled, curling on itself, a lazy smile spreading as he retrieved the bag.

I am convinced Showboat should not have given away whatever was in the bag.

Ginny sucks in a breath and rereads the passage. What had Showboat been passing on to the *non*-American, *non*-reporter? All of Egypt was nothing if not a hotbed of spies and counterspies. Given Showboat's tendency to thumb his nose at authority and do whatever was best for himself, she wouldn't put it past him to do something stupid.

And both Cliff and Nikos seemed to think Showboat was being shifty.

She'd seen Showboat a day or two ago. After another infraction of some kind, he was reassigned to push papers at headquarters. Where he would have more access to even more information he can pass on to this Monkaster...if that's what Showboat was doing. She imagined his stiff face as he sat behind the desk, filing papers for his father.

If Showboat is passing information on to Monkaster, he'd do anything to protect himself.

What if Cliff had uncovered something that had gotten him killed? And if Showboat is involved, had he killed poor Argus? Had he done something to Cliff's plane?

Ginny clenches the pendant as if the red stone will lend her wisdom or protection. The blunt edges dig into her skin, the warmth nearly burning her palm. What in the world is she to do? If Showboat is responsible, the barbed wire fence and guards can't keep the enemy out. The traitors are already inside.

Night coils around the tent, bringing the hot breath of the sky goddess Nut as she swallows the sun. Somewhere in the camp, a woman keens, raising the hairs on Ginny's arms. She, admittedly, had had zero interest in the Egyptian myths or culture before being planted in the Red Desert for months on end. But in the dark, as she thinks about Showboat's weird meeting at the restaurant, Cliff going down in the desert, that strange snake man...she can't help but feel like Apophis is circling the entire world, opening his snake-like mouth to devour them all.

Strangely, the Egyptian Apophis myth is the one story that paints the god Set as anything other than chaos and death and betrayal. He is one of the few gods strong enough to defeat the serpent.

Her stomach churns with all that Cliff kept from her. Why hadn't he said anything? No doubt trying to protect her...like she was some delicate debutante. What was it her sister called her nemeses? The Hog Princesses? Well, Ginny is not a Hog Princess nor is she a coward.

The wailing drops into a repetitive chant, and Ginny wonders who is at death's door. What spell is the chanter weaving? Will it work? Like Aset, can the woman bring the dead back to life? Ginny wraps her hand around the necklace, closing her eyes to imagine that she can still feel Cliff's fingers holding the pendant.

A tear drops onto the journal page, another streaking to join it, curling into one another for comfort. But where can anyone find comfort when your arms are empty, and the enemy is closing in?

6

I unbury my master's spear from the coils of the cold-blooded beast and stumble to my knees. As my form slides from beast to human, the red sand claws at my eyes and my skin. I am weary of the struggle against this serpent.

I pass the woman's tent and drag a hand over the doorway, passing through a moment, watching her study the pages.

Relief settles across my shoulders. Perhaps she can help where I am no longer able. While I can fight otherworldly things, I am bound and cannot destroy those who have slid onto the mortal plane. She has the pendant, and it should protect her if she listens.

Tears prick my eyes. I swipe them away in a mirror of her movements...for a different reason. Yet in our humanity, we are the same. Water falls when we're happy or sad or overwhelmed. When we miss someone, when we see them again. When we have hope, and when we lose it. We have a need for another language, but since we don't have one, we're cursed to make do with the words and motions we do have. Cursed to bend to the whims of the gods to find what we most need. A safe place to sleep, water to drink. The promise of a tomorrow, if not for our sakes, then for our children's.

And I have seen my future children—Saira, Mehedi. Know that there will be little rest for them either. Set, as he weaves the human wars, will destroy most of us, including me, and I cannot see beyond. He is necessary, for now.

Yet there will be a woman like this one who will stand between the world and Set. I pray she will declare victory.

And so, I hug my black robes against me as I pass back through the door, chanting the words of Aset's protection and ducking away before Horus suspects my interference. He will never believe that in this, I, a woman enslaved to the god of chaos, and he are allies.

7

———————

The sound of careful footsteps nearby propels a half-asleep Ginny to her feet. Had someone been inside the tent? Carlotta is on shift. When the steps continue unabated past her, Ginny slumps in relief, then scrambles to gather the scattered journals, her pillow, and...she hesitates. Cliff's journal is splayed open to a horrifying collision of random words, a scratchy image of a serpent, sketches of falcon eyes, flames, and a final line: "Apophis has won and the only way to save them is—" A dark smudge follows the words.

Ginny flips the page, looking for the end of the sentence, but the rest of the little book is empty.

What in the world? This did not sound like Cliff.

The bunk shudders, and Ginny stills. There is almost no wind to speak of this morning, and the unexpectedness of the movement presses against her lungs. She pokes her head out from behind the screen, and her gaze sweeps the interior, wondering if maybe the steps she'd heard really were someone inside as she'd first thought.

But everything is as it should be—four bunks made with tight hospital corners, a cramped desk, and a wooden chair. Even the little cross above the door is steady.

Maybe someone bumped into the wall, exhausted or drunk on the way home.

Ginny rubs the pressure building behind the bridge of her nose. The odd entry makes Ginny wonder: If he'd survived the crash, where was he now? And why would someone go through the effort of delivering the journal to her? If the Army had found the crash and the journal, wouldn't they have sent it back to Iowa? Why was it here? And why had a Bedouin woman delivered it?

She turns back to the smudge and brings the book closer to her nose. There's a swirling pattern in the dark blot. A fingerprint? It's smeared enough Ginny can't be sure. If she needs to confirm that this is Cliff's journal, all the pilots were fingerprinted, and this at least could prove who wrote it. It's something at least.

She flips back to what she skipped last night. He'd followed the supposed journalist, watching as he talked to Allied soldiers, traipsing between Groppi's, Shepheard's Hotel, the Kit-Kat Club, anywhere strangers' paths crossed. It was a mind-numbing array of boring lists of dates and times and people, but then...

> *I'd thought Monkaster was a wealthy socialite slumming with the riffraff. But tonight, I learned the truth. I stood on the seawall close enough to Monkaster's houseboat that I could hear him talking to a woman. She was hollering loud enough that my sister back in Iowa would've handed her a wrench and told her to fix her attitude. I could only catch bits and pieces, but sure as shooting, he's caught up in some kind of ring calling itself Apophis. And put that together with the folks he's been talking to, the stories he keeps shifting, and the fact that he seems to be trading in information and not goods, I think this Monkaster is an Axis spy.*

A thud booms from just outside the door, and Ginny leaps to her feet, combat knife in hand.

Carlotta trudges into the tent and comes up short with a gasp.

"Sorry." Ginny lets her arm fall to her side.

"Rough night?" Carlotta's words sound relaxed, but as she slips behind the first bunk, her posture is alert, tense, watching.

"Something like that," Ginny hedges.

Carlotta's eyes slip to Ginny's tangled nighttime nest and then back to Ginny, who's probably more of a disaster now than she was the day after she'd heard Cliff's plane had gone down. Ginny straightens her pajama shirt and tucks an unruly strand of dark hair behind her ear. She's buying time, trying to figure out what to say, what to hold back. If she tells Carlotta, is she putting her friend in danger?

Carlotta pushes away from the bunk, her eyes never leaving her friend's, until she lifts Ginny's hand and slips out first the knife, then the journal.

Ginny slumps to sit on her bunk, watching Carlotta read. Her best friend's face changes from sadness to horror to absolute confusion in a bizarre parody of Ginny's own emotions.

"I don't know what to think," Ginny says when she can't stand the quiet anymore.

"Did you know any of this?" Carlotta waves a hand over the pages, as if the motion might make sensical words appear.

Ginny shakes her head.

"If this is true, he couldn't have trusted anyone at the base, considering Showboat's father is Lieutenant Colonel Albert Ames."

Ginny drops her face into her hands. Lieutenant Colonel Ames, head of U.S. Army Intelligence in Cairo.

Cliff had been terrified for Ginny, for himself, for the war.

"This has to be why he volunteered for the delivery run. So he could inform officers outside the base."

"Oh, Ginny." Carlotta eases next to her friend.

Ginny leans onto her shoulder, no tears left.

Carlotta lets out an impressive string of curses in at least five languages, which just makes Ginny laugh and say, "Exactly."

"Did he find any real evidence?"

"Not that I've read about yet."

"What are you going to do?"

"I have no idea." She takes the journal back from Carlotta and flips through the pages, scanning. For what she doesn't know. "Would it have been too much to ask him to write, 'Read this page for the answers'?"

Carlotta leans over, elbows on her knees, and peers back at her friend. "Well, I know I'm not going to let Monkaster or Showboat get away with this. Let's unleash a whole load of mayhem. Your daddy's got friends, doesn't he? And there's got to be evidence in the plane?"

"They didn't find it."

Carlotta bolts to her feet. "What?"

"The plane. They still haven't found it."

"Then how did you get this?" Carlotta lifts the package and gives a dry laugh, sharp and cutting as the desert stones.

Ginny swallows. And the words flood out. "A Bedouin woman delivered it."

Carlotta's mouth works, but the words are slow to slog through what Ginny recognizes as the quicksand of confusion. "I thought they found his plane and this and...what else aren't you telling me?"

Ginny rubs a hand across her face, feeling the grit of the desert embedded in her skin, her hair, under her nails, in every crevasse of her being. Grime she was beginning to think she would never be rid of. "Argus misreported the location of the crash site."

"He misreported the crash site? I thought you trusted him."

"He was trying to protect Cliff. At least that's what he said. He said I was in danger, and he blames it all on Showboat and—" Confusion and fear choke off the rest of the sentence in a weak, sobbing squeak. When had she become a scared little mouse? "What am I going to do?"

"Well, if that jerk Showboat is involved, we certainly can't let him realize we know anything."

"Which means we have to act normal...which is what I've been trying to do. But..." Ginny hugs the journal against her chest. "Do you think Cliff dreamed it all up?"

"Cliff?" Carlotta laughs until she realizes Ginny is serious and puts a hand on each shoulder so she can look her friend dead in the eyes. "That man was one of the most stable, put-together people I know. And I know a lot of people, honey."

"You didn't read the end." Ginny opens the notebook to the crash date and hands the book to her friend.

As Carlotta's eyebrows bunch, the terror rises in Ginny again. She knows what's there. She read the words last night, but somehow they transported her into the scene as if she were living it herself.

I know that I have a good-sized gash on my forehead. But it ain't nothing worse than anything else I've had to deal with. My dad's brother once fell into a table saw. His gut was cut open, and he survived. So I reckon I can as well.

The wind continues to ravage the hollow I've found. I wonder how my Warhawk is faring. She wasn't made for Egyptian sandstorms. Until last night, the cracked cockpit glass had blunted the worst of the sand, but a steadily growing river flowed through.

With little left in my canteen, I put a note with my plans in the Sky King. I was able to unstick my compass and pry it up with my knife. The quartermaster will have my hide for damaging my plane further, but it was my life or a few dents in the Sky King.

Yesterday, I stumbled through the storm for hours, so turned around I was sure I was going to die. But then, as ridiculous as it sounds, a path opened in front of me, guiding me to the steps that led to a decent-sized burial chamber. I stumbled down the steps, grateful for a safe place to sleep.

This morning, reality has sunk in. I'm lost. I haven't slept much. And I know that is affecting my thoughts. I am stuck here with little food and no water. Unless something changes, I can't afford to set out again.

This afternoon, I have a bit of hope. The dust storm may be letting up some. Not only that, but I have found an abandoned tent to bed down for tonight. It seems to be rather new, which makes me hopeful that in the morning I might be able to find people nearby. Someone had to have left the tent behind.

I don't know if Showboat and Argus made it out or if they were able to take an accurate dead reckoning of where I went down. The idea of finding my way back to you keeps my hope alive.

In some ways, I wish I had never set out on this fool's

journey to uncover the Apophis spies. What information could lackeys like Showboat really be giving whoever Monkaster is working for? But if I refuse to stick my neck out for others, what does that make me?

My uncle used to tell Robbie Jane and me all kinds of stories of the uprisings in Ireland, going all the way back to the days of the Tuatha Dé Danann, the queens and kings and bards and healers that were the powerful ancestors of the Little People. Despite the odds, they fought against their enemies, and the moment they stopped, they lost most of their powers and hid under the hills...or at least that's Uncle Paddy's take. That they were cowards in the end. And the last thing I want to be is a coward.

When I'd heard that I was shipping to Egypt, my friend Moe went to the library and checked out every book he could about the place and summarized it all for me in a letter that was nearly the size of a book itself. But he's the one who told me to be like Horus. The falcon god of justice and order. The Sky King. And yet, here I am, buried and useless like the Little People.

Carlotta's voice cracks against Cliff's pain, cutting off her reading and jarring Ginny from the swirl of sand in her mind's eye.

"That poor man," Carlotta whispers, breaking into a language Ginny doesn't understand. But the sentiment is there—anger, confusion.

Ginny leans against her friend's shoulder, glad she isn't the only one dealing with a chaotic storm of feelings. "Are you okay?"

"Me?" Carlotta huffs. "I should be the one asking you that."

"It gets worse."

"Oh, honey. I'm sorry."

"Keep reading."

Carlotta sucks in an enormous gulp of air, but there isn't enough oxygen in the entire world to brace her. Ginny stands, shakes out her hands, then leans against the bunk, eyes closed.

Last night I found a bit of sleep, and that has let me think more clearly. I know you have seen the results of a man who has been stuck out in a sandstorm before. I am sure that I resemble the headless Dullahan from my uncle's tales. As if an Irish monster could survive this blasted desert.

However, the Valley of the Kings has been kind to this Iowa farm boy, and I have found refuge in what appears to be an abandoned pharaoh's tomb. It's very kind of the pharaoh to invite me in. Don't you think?

I wish you were here, though only if accompanied by a rescue team. My face feels on fire from the thorough sanding. It's no wonder that my poor P-40 could not continue. Which makes me think that I could do with both you and my sister here. You to fix my face. And my sister to fix the Sky King. I seem to be the only one in my family who can't take two paper clips and make an engine out of them.

We made a good team back home, my sister and I. Her tinkering with the engines and me racing her creations.

Here I am pining for home, completely forgetting to tell you that I found a bit of condensation at the back of the tomb and left my canteen to collect the droplets. After using a Hala-zone tablet, I had enough water to slake my thirst, even if it burned like bleach and stone dust.

In the moments when the wind slows down, I can see shadows on the horizon, which make me think there is a settle-ment nearby, and if my comrades are not back by nightfall, I will turn that way to seek help. I have spent about an hour directing SOS signals toward the shadow with my flashlight, and I believe I have seen an answer. By my next entry, my dearest Virginia, I pray that you will have heard of my safe arrival.

Midday, a thud sent me scrambling in hopes that someone

had found me, but to my chagrin, the wind had merely knocked over a statue of the falcon-headed Horus. Do you remember the stories I told you about Horus and his uncle, Set? I can't help but think that the Egyptians were crazy to believe that someone who created storms like this was necessary.

What if everyone simply befriended everyone else? What would happen then?

I found a series of steps leading down into the tomb. A yawning doorway. My sister would be convinced that hell was just beyond the opening. After another night here listening to the groans of the stone around me, I'm as jumpy as my little sister with thoughts of the Ticky Man chasing her. There was a moment when I swear I watched darkness slide into my skin. I'm sure it was just dirt or shadows, but there are other things. The Horus statue that fell last night is gone. Not broken to dust on the ground but completely disappeared. And now I hear voices, words slipping through the rocks with the condensation.

I'm determined to leave today. It seems ridiculous, but I've come to think that—one flyer to another—Horus's falcon statue was trying to warn me. I hear the hiss of Apophis stalking, the clang of Set's spear. In trying to destroy the beast, Set may very well destroy us all.

I woke to a Bedouin woman bending over me, dripping water into my mouth. Her strange eyes flickered in the red light. I didn't know what time it was let alone what day. I'd set out to find the village and wandered for what seemed like days. I had thought I would die. I don't remember being rescued.

A fire flickered between us and a hulking tent. She told me to be quiet or risk the wrath of Apophis. She nodded toward a circle of men, and I realized they were the ring of traitors. I think one of them may have been Showboat. The one nearest me growled at the woman, pointing to the edge of the camp. His sleeve slipped back, and I'm certain he had a snake tattooed on his wrist. His eyes snapped to me and then the woman, a string of angry commands as he thrust himself to his feet. But the woman waved a hand at him—a clear command to sit and be quiet.

He looked to challenge her, but the air shifted, and she lifted her head, listening.

Then she tucked the flask under my arm, stood, and dove into a swirling of dust. I caught a bare glimpse, but I saw a strange form with tall square ears and a swishing forked tail. There was a clash of metal, a snarling, and then quiet.

I scrambled to my elbows, backing away as a creature bayed in victory. I turned to my hands and knees and scrambled into the dark. Then, I believed I'd been delivered into the hands of Lord Set himself.

This morning, I woke to quiet, and I don't know what to think. The woman is back, but the men are gone. She is grim and covered in blood that she says is from a snake. But I don't think there's a snake big enough in the desert for the amount on her. It's more than I've seen in the slaughterhouse. Ginny, I know it sounds crazy, but I think she's complicit with Set if not the traitors. I don't think I'm going to survive the day. I am sorry, my love. I—

"I don't understand." Carlotta points to the series of random numbers and strange hieroglyphic images that follow the end of the words and trailing smudge.

"I don't either."

Carlotta traces her finger over the page, her finger snagging on a place where Cliff had underlined a series of numbers so hard that the page had torn under the pressure. Carlotta frowns, thinking. "You said

Argus misreported the crash site?"

Ginny nods.

"Do you know where the right location is?"

Ginny digs out Argus's note. Carlotta takes it and smooths it over the series of numbers in Cliff's journal. Leaning over to see what Carlotta is studying, Ginny realizes that there's also a small circle above the last of the numbers. "Coordinates?"

Carlotta grins at her friend. "I think so."

Hope rises full and free, except..."What are we supposed to do with this? Cliff didn't trust anyone here, which means we can't either."

"We can kidnap Showboat, tie the creep up, and make him talk." Carlotta's grin is wicked enough that Ginny's half convinced she's being serious.

"With who his dad is? I don't want to be court martialed."

Carlotta sits back with a grumble about what she'd like to do to the low-down, no-good, spoiled lout. It may or may not have involved a syringe, a dark hallway, and a shot of something he wouldn't soon forget.

Ginny laughs. "If my brother was here, he'd figure out a way to get Showboat to talk, but I'm more likely to join you with that syringe than talk to him." She paces the tent, then whips around with an idea. "You sure you don't know anyone who can help?"

"What are you—"

"All the soldiers who've come and gone have to know someone who could help. The new one is a British officer, right? Could he get us to MI6?" The Brits would be more likely to investigate Showboat than a US officer who reports to his father.

A fly drones through the tent, and Carlotta swats it away as she thinks. Ginny knows she's stalling, but no one gets anywhere by pushing Carlotta.

"I have leave today." Carlotta stands. "You do too, right?"

At Ginny's nod, Carlotta sweeps behind the screen, and a moment later, her uniform drops over the carved wood, and she steps out in a smart traveling costume—a pinstriped dress with a wing collar so sharply pressed, it bordered on miraculous.

Ginny scrambles to her feet. "What are you doing?"

"I do believe you're friends with the baker at Groppo's, yes?"

Ginny feels like she has stuffed animal brains. All fluff and no function. "What does Nikos have to do with this?"

Carlotta shifts her weight and juts out a semi-patient hip. "If Showboat was talking to this Monkaster fellow at Groppo's, other people probably are too. If we go talk to your friend, maybe he'll be able to tell us more."

Thus, the traveling clothes. They're off to Cairo.

"I'll pop down to the motor pool and see about a car." Carlotta pats her friend's arm like she might pat a pet dog who might be rabid. "You do something about"—she waves her hand over Ginny's general person"—and maybe run a brush through your hair?"

Ginny raises a sharp eyebrow but refrains from saying what she's thinking: Who has time to primp when her world is falling apart?

"You know as well as I do that folks will judge you. If you look like you're panicking and falling apart, they are far less likely to listen."

"Everyone likes a happy person," Ginny snaps.

"No one *questions* a happy person."

"And there's no room for grief or pain or the messy business of finding justice." Jaw clenched, Ginny yanks a brush through her matted locks.

"We'll find out what happened, Ginny. Just..." Carlotta sucks in a deep breath, her eyes, which find her friend's, brimming with tears. "Just be prepared for news you don't want to hear."

Ginny's hands tighten around the journal. She hadn't heard the phrase in months. The reminder between friends that they lived in a war zone. Nothing and no one could be depended on. Not because they didn't want to show up, but because sometimes they couldn't. Ginny goes back to detangling her hair, letting the brush rip at her scalp, punishing herself for allowing hope to return. She is a combat war nurse, able and prepared for a literal bomb to be dropped outside her door.

Her fingers twist her tresses into a tight bun before she strips off her sweaty nightclothes, throws on a random shirt, skirt, and hat, then pops out the door right into the wavering form of the Bedouin woman.

8

Ginny sucks in a hissing breath. "You!"

The woman's sharp fingers clamp around Ginny's arm. "Where are you going?" She looks over Ginny's shoulder.

Ginny follows her look. A bird flutters on the roof of the barracks across the way. If a look could incinerate, the bird would be a pile of ash.

Ginny smashes the notebooks against her body. "Not that you care or have any ground to ask, we're going to take this to a friend. He'll help us find Cliff's plane and Cliff and—"

"He's dead." The woman's eyes are hard, a flicker of molten stone.

Ginny blanches. The bird fluffs, drawing both women's attention. The Bedouin woman's visage flickers. Ginny swears she sees the predatory face of a wild animal, and she yanks backward. But the woman holds tight.

"I do not wish to be cruel. But I will not allow you to ruin what I have set in motion, what your Cliff set in motion. Even the falcon dares not interfere."

"The falcon?" What in the world is she talking about? Ginny squints at the bird like it might explain the crazy woman.

"Do not interfere."

"Then why did you give me this?" Ginny's voice is high, tinged with frustration, grief, and fear.

"Apophis is in the camp. I tried—" The Bedouin woman glances over her shoulder, then flickers back. "Your Cliff was about to strike the tail of the snake. His spear would not cut the iron hide. Horus cannot defeat the cursed creature. But Aset?" The woman reaches forward and brushes against the pendant around Ginny's neck. "She holds the strongest magic, and we might do together what I cannot do alone."

Ginny smacks the woman's hand away. "What in the name of all that is holy are you talking about? I already know Apophis is here. I'm not—"

"I know nothing." Her chin snaps up, listening. "I must go." She turns, floating around the corner with such grace and speed Ginny's mind can't quite make sense of her movements. The bird launches himself from the roof, banking after the strange woman.

"Well." Carlotta's voice from behind makes Ginny jump. "That was odd."

"Yeah."

"I'm assuming she's the one who gave you the journal. What do you want to do?" Carlotta's question snaps Ginny's attention from the shadows, and she turns to her friend.

Carlotta nods, still watching the place where the woman had disappeared.

"Do you think they killed Cliff over this?" Ginny lifts the journal.

When her friend doesn't respond, Ginny touches her arm, and Carlotta startles like she's been stung.

♀

AFTER CARLOTTA BATS her impressively long lashes, the soldier manning the motor pool hands over keys for a Jeep. Carlotta promptly presses them into Ginny's hand with an "adorable boy doesn't realize that no self-respecting Abrams woman drives herself anywhere."

Ginny stifles a laugh and strides through the row of Jeeps. She and Carlotta slip into the vehicle, and Ginny starts the engine. It's been months since she's driven, but Chicago made sure she was proficient enough to navigate onto the new tarmac.

With the windows open, dust swirls into the Jeep, gathering in every crease and crevice. At least she'll have good reason for her wild locks. She can practically feel abrasions forming with every movement. The heat and anxiety don't help. Nor does Carlotta's happy humming. And by the time they reach Helliopis, a storm is brewing beneath Ginny's normally placid demeanor. When another donkey cart stops in the middle of the road for no apparent reason, Ginny pounds on the horn. Every single passenger on the overly packed bus next to them frowns in her direction.

Carlotta places a steadying hand on Ginny's shoulder. "I know you're jumping out of your skin. But I'd like to get there in one piece if that's okay with you." She hollers over the din of the engine and the mass of humanity.

"Does this blasted country know how to do anything other than chaos?" Ginny growls.

"Aren't you from Chicago?" Carlotta giggles.

"There are rules in Chicago." She swerves around a man in a fine, tailored suit who stepped into the street as if he owned it, and then slams on her brakes for a random cart in the road.

"There are rules here too."

"That no one seems to be obeying. And"—Ginny curses at the complacent long-eared animal who nips at the Jeep's bumper in return. "There aren't donkeys in Chicago. Or their dung."

"No. But there are taxi drivers, and we won't find help if we run over the locals." Carlotta nudges her friend's shoulder. Ginny sucks in a deep breath. Carlotta is right. No matter how she wishes to control the entire street, she hasn't been assigned the role of God or even the abilities of a superhero like Wonder Woman.

Her fingers trail over the pendant nestled between her collarbones. "Do you know who Aset is?"

"The goddess of magic and healing?" Carlotta's voice rises in question over the abrupt change in subject.

"Yeah, but I mean all that stuff about raising her husband from the dead and saving her son."

"She was supposed to be the ultimate role model of motherhood because she saved Horus. I've sometimes wondered if it was fair of her though."

"Fair of her to what? Save her son?" Ginny blares the horn at a goat wandering on the street and mutters under her breath about bringing roadkill to Nikos as tribute, and she almost misses Carlotta sighing, "If he hadn't survived, there wouldn't have been war."

"That's awfully fatalistic. Not to mention that if Horus hadn't survived, we'd be left with the straight-up chaos of Set."

"But chaos will never give up."

"Then neither should we, right?" They finally burst through the city limits of the town and onto the relatively wide-open stretch of road. Though covered in a fine layer of sand, the pavement underneath is relatively new (thanks to the Allies) and relatively unscathed from bombings. Ginny's heart races with the possibility that they may soon know what happened to Cliff. She chides herself for letting hope rise, but, despite the Bedouin woman's assertions, her shiftiness and her obvious desire to escape questions make Ginny question the veracity of her claim that Cliff is dead. Maybe Nikos will know more.

9

———————

Thirty minutes later, they're finally in Cairo and Ginny swings down Qasr El Nil Street, bursting into neon lights, elegant shops, and an odd mix of Allied uniforms and Arabic dress. And then finally, blessedly, they roll into Talaat Harb Square, where Groppi's sits glittering with its famous art nouveau facade. Ginny swings into a spot that's mostly too short for the Jeep, turns off the vehicle, and shoves herself out of the vehicle.

"Hold on there, killer." Carlotta is swiping on fresh lipstick and fluffing her somehow still perfectly coifed hair.

"We don't have time to—"

"Do you think the men in there will give you the time of day if they think you're off your rocker?"

Ginny blinks at her friend, her core wanting to walk away on principle. But Carlotta raises an eyebrow, and Ginny concedes, slapping her hand out for the blasted lipstick. Carlotta hands over the brightest red lipstick Ginny has ever seen. She hesitates a moment under the raised brows of her fellow nurse, carefully lines her lips, then turns to her friend. "Is this sufficient, mother?"

"Now do something with your hair." Carlotta digs a brush from her cavernous bag, and Ginny gapes into the overstuffed thing.

"Did you pack an overnight bag?"

"One can never be too careful or too overprepared."

Ginny yanks the brush through her hair yet again, taming it back into the serviceable chignon.

"You'll do." Carlotta loops her arm through Ginny's and swings her friend around the lampposts, past the bright floral mosaics, and into the doorway.

When a GI opens the door for the women, the smell of sweet pastries and ice cream nearly makes Ginny's knees collapse with hunger. When is the last time she ate? Carlotta pats the GI's arm in thanks and sashays into the room like a queen, leaving Ginny to stumble behind her like a forgotten nursemaid. The rolling rumble of conversation doesn't hesitate, though, and Ginny sighs despite herself. She misses Cliff lighting up every time she walks into a room. No, she's not the most gorgeous creature to walk the planet. But he seemed to disagree and balanced out her no-nonsense drill sergeant life. She misses him swinging her into a dance to music only he could hear, telling her the most ridiculous jokes just to stop her catastrophizing. Was he overconfident sometimes? Of course. It's why he thought he could take down a spy ring on his own. He was a pilot. It's what pilots did.

Was? Ginny clutches her skirt, her mind recreating the Bedouin woman's piercing voice. *He's dead.* Her lungs burn, and she inhales, forcing herself to breathe. She's terrified he's dead, but to be absolutely sure might destroy her. No, she reminds herself of the woman's darting eyes and clipped tone. The woman could easily have been lying.

As the pair step aside to allow another GI into the room, Ginny can feel eyes on them and turns. In the back, several men stare at her, like they're trying to figure out where they've seen her before. Ginny slips her arm through her friend's elbow and leans in. "Carlotta, can you do something about them?" She nods surreptitiously at the men.

"Aren't we trying to be clandestine?" Carlotta whispers loudly.

Ginny laughs, light and tinkling. "And if they're looking at you, they will hardly be paying attention to what I'm doing or asking now, will they?"

Carlotta gives a wicked grin, then weaves through the tables under the crystal chandeliers, finger-waving at a table of men wearing disheveled suits and sporting notebooks. Reporters. Ginny merely nods as their attention bumps to her, then back to Carlotta, who's ordering a bowl of ice cream.

"You are amazing," Ginny whispers.

"I didn't get where I am by not using what the good Lord gave me, sweetheart. You know as well as I do folks see what they want to see. It takes a special person to look deeper and find the truth. I suggest you go talk to Nikos and whoever else you need to, and I'll work my magic out here so that no one realizes what you're up to."

As Carlotta accepts her bowl of ice cream, she carefully lifts the slice of mango on top and pops it between her cherry-red lips. She saunters over to the reporters whose attention fixes on the pretty woman approaching them, allowing Ginny to slip unseen into the back hallway. She clenches and releases her fingers, anesthetizing her out-of-control emotions. She pushes through the swinging doors.

In the stark white kitchen, Nikos is bent over a bowl, his arm muscles straining against the weight of the batter. Ginny clears her throat, and the baker startles, nearly dropping both bowl and spoon. At the sight of her, he swallows. Though he smiles, it's a moment too late, and the flick of his eyes to the dining room signals fear.

"No one saw me come back here." Ginny leans against a wall, far from prying eyes and the windows in the door.

While Nikos goes back to work, dumping the dough onto a floured surface, his movements are stiff, completely lacking the earlier grace. Ginny has no idea where to start, no idea how much Nikos knows, no idea where any of the danger might be. But she cannot do nothing. Cliff had written to her, told her his story.

"Cliff sent me his journal."

Niko's movements hiccup but don't stop.

"Argus said he lied about where Cliff's plane went down to try to protect him." Ginny hesitates, weighing what might snap Nikos out of his pretend detachment. "They're both dead. And they were both scared I'm in danger. And if I'm in danger..."

Nikos stills, his hands hovering over the pastry dough. A woman in the dining room laughs. A man's overconfident voice answers.

"The only way we can all be safe is if we stop whatever is going on. I have evidence that there is a ring of traitors, but I don't know who is running everything. And I can't safely turn over the documentation if I'm not sure we have the identities of all the traitors I don't even know who not to tell." Ginny pushes away from the wall. "You and your family aren't safe either, Nikos. You have to know that. Will you tell me what you know?"

Nikos looks up from his sagging dough. "I can only tell you what I suspect. There's a man who says he is Peter Monkaster, an American reporter. But his story does not always work, you know? He lives on a boat down at the docks. He asks too many questions, and his story? It isn't right. He says he's from Chicago and sometimes from all over, and other times he evades." Nikos punches down the dough. "But no one listens to Nikos, do they?"

"Cliff said you don't think he's American. And I believe you too." Ginny gives him a sad smile in exchange for the lift of his broad shoulders.

"See that it does not kill us both, huh?"

Ginny swallows down the fear, slapping determination over top of it. Her life has been threatened before. You can't work in an inner-city Chicago mission without facing a knife or two. Mostly she let her brother, Marcus, talk them out of trouble. But between Cliff and Marcus, she's had enough lessons that she should be able to verbally evade danger now. Maybe. "Is he here now?"

Gesturing with his chin, Nikos points through the kitchen window to a table wedged into the back corner, exactly where Carlotta has planted herself across from a dark-haired man in a too neat, too tailored cream linen suit.

Ginny bows, hands pressed together in a sign of both prayer and thanks, but before she can duck out the door, Nikos presents her with a plate. "Take this." He drizzles a thin white glaze on top and nods solemnly in a benediction of sorts. "Egyptian Quince Cake."

Tears prick at Ginny's eyes. "Thank you." With Cliff's invention in hand, Ginny slides into the dining room and slips next to Carlotta. "Compliments of the chef." She sets the dessert between them, then looks up, feigning delighted surprise. "Oh! I'm sorry, I'll—"

"No need." The man's studying her, and Ginny does her best to relax. He can't recognize her. She's never met him before.

"This is Mr. Peter Monkaster." Carlotta takes an enormous forkful of the dessert and shoves it into her mouth, somehow making the indulgence look like the height of desirable fashion. She moans and then swallows. "He's from...say what newspaper again?"

"I'm a stringer."

"A stringer?" Carlotta hums with flirtation. "I like the sound of that."

Monkaster chuckles. "It means I write for many newspapers. Whoever will pay me."

Ginny fights to keep a neutral face. His accent isn't bad per se, but he's missing the sharp, fast, no-nonsense attitude of most big city reporters. Plus, tailored suits are more affordable in Cairo, to be sure, but what he's wearing isn't normal for a regular correspondent, let alone a stringer. None of which is enough to convict the man.

"How in the world did you find your way into that?" Ginny pours as much of Carlotta's flirting into her voice as she dares. "It sounds ever so dangerous in a war zone."

"I kind of fell into it. My father wanted me to be a businessman, but I never could make numbers line themselves."

"I know exactly what you mean." Ginny smiles, letting her dimples show. "I always have to triple-check my numbers before I push a dose. Morphine's not something you want to get wrong. Can you imagine the paperwork?"

Carlotta stiffens next to her. Ginny has never and will never make a mistake in her numbers. Ginny concentrates on taking a tiny bite of the dessert, not expecting to notice much of anything, but flavor bursts on her tongue, and she can't help echoing Carlotta's moan.

Carlotta gives a little giggle and nudges her friend. "You need to get out more often." Then she turns her overly bright smile on Monkaster. "Do you have any suggestions?"

Monkaster goes red, his eyes flickering to his manicured hands, strangely absent of ink. "With you, I would love to show the town."

Carlotta looks at Ginny with a little shrug. Ginny nods with an "I guess that's one way to talk to him" raise of her eyebrows.

Carlotta claps like a happy toddler. "You can ride with us, sugar."

She winds her hand through Ginny's elbow. They need a plan before loading a spy into the backseat of the Jeep. Ginny slowly takes another bite of the cake. There's nowhere to take him in the city, is there? And it isn't like they can tie him up in the backseat and interrogate him.

There's morphine in the Jeep's medical kit. Sometimes folks got chatty when they were drugged. But why would he roll up his sleeve and—

Ginny smiles and carefully straightens the table before standing. Germans have different inoculation scars. If they can get the man to show his upper arm, they'll know for sure. But how?

Carlotta is fawning over the man, and Ginny realizes that hewants nothing more than for them to worship the ground he walks on. He has no idea what a woman is capable of. And if Aset can raise the dead, she can corner this fool.

Ginny leans over. "He's welcome to join us, but the tire is shot."

Carlotta blinks at her, trying to decode the message. "The tire—?"

"Needs changing." Ginny raises her eyebrows and slides out of the booth before anyone can object.

Carlotta stumbles out behind her, dragging Monkaster, like a puppy, in her wake.

When the women arrive at the Jeep, Ginny strides to the passenger side, pulls Cliff's knife from her handbag, and leans down. The sudden sharp hiss is covered by the braying of a donkey. At least the foul things are helpful for something.

"See?" Cool as the ice cream, Ginny points to the ruined tire. "The Army doesn't seem to be able to provide tires that can survive this heat. Do you think you can help, sugar?"

Puffed up like a peacock, Monkaster struts to the back of the Jeep, unloads the wrench, and yanks at the lugs holding on the spare. In her mind, Ginny can't help hearing Cliff say that he wished his sister was with him. Roberta Jane would have that tire off lickety-split. But poor Monkaster is melting.

Finally catching on to the plan, Carlotta flutters around him, not helping one iota until she says, "Let me hold your jacket, sugar. You don't want that getting damaged."

He frowns but shrugs out of the cream coat and hands it to Ginny.

"Oh!" Ginny fans herself, feeling ridiculous. "Don't you just love a man's forearms, Carlotta?" If she can just get him to roll up his sleeves...

Carlotta plasters her face with bewildered agreement, which seems to soothe Monkaster, who unexpectedly rolls up his sleeves. When he goes back to work, Ginny frowns as she maneuvers around the man, trying to look at his biceps.

And that's when Carlotta obviously realizes the rest of Ginny's plan. Carlotta catches her friend's thinking frown and mouths *Help him.*

Help him? She doesn't know how to—

Suddenly Carlotta gives a little yelp and stumbles over the curb, bumping into Monkaster so that the lug wrench slips and slashes across his shoulder. Carlotta widens her eyes at Ginny, a plea for distraction.

She spins perhaps a moment too late and hollers at no one in particular, "Hey! Watch it!" Then turns back to a bleeding Monkaster who is soothing Carlotta.

"Are you two okay? Those two jerks just about ran you over." Ginny throws another look over her shoulder for good measure.

Carlotta eases to the curb, stars in her eyes for her rescuing hero. She's laying it on a little thick, but Monkaster is gobbling up every morsel.

"Mr. Monkaster saved me."

"But you earned yourself a nasty gash." Ginny pouts about the minor scratch, hating the helpless nurse act. "We can't let you go to one of the hospitals around here. I have a kit. Let me just fetch it and I'll—"

"It's fine," Monkaster says. "Just fine."

But Ginny's already digging in the backseat for the medical kit. "It wouldn't be Christian of me to let you go without examining it." She snatches the canvas bag and extracts herself from the back of the Jeep. Monkaster is busy watching Carlotta test her ankle and distractedly complies with Ginny's request for him to roll up his shirt sleeves so she can get a better look.

Ginny deftly takes hold of his elbow and pushes his sleeve up a hair higher than strictly necessary, and Monkaster flinches like he's been stung.

She is all empty-headed apologies for hurting him further, but she's seen exactly what she needed to. Any American would have a single neat, round scar high on the upper arm. But this man's scar is a ragged constellation of pitted marks etched into his arm—a literal Wermacht branding. Monkaster isn't an American anything.

Ginny makes quick work of cleaning the scratch with iodine then covers it with gauze and tape.

"If you haven't had a recent tetanus shot, you should come with us."

Carlotta is suddenly on her feet. "Oh! Do come. We'll be able to"—she flashes a wicked grin—"make sure you're cared for. We'll set everything to rights."

If this man is looking for information about the Allied base, he won't be able to pass up the opportunity to spy on them directly.

The last thing Ginny really wants is a traitor in the Jeep for the hour drive back to the base, especially since she still doesn't know who to tell about Cliff's suspicions or her confirmation that the man parading as an American journalist is, instead German as Berlin. Surely the MPs will listen to her if she literally brings evidence of Apophis to their feet. Won't they?

"We'll just give you like a little something for the pain and be on our way. Sound good, hon?" Carlotta's already grabbing a red and white morphine syrette from the kit and barely waits for Monkaster to nod absently before she pops off the plastic cover and injects the liquid.

Carlotta waves Monkaster into the backseat, leaving Ginny to finish changing the tire and climb warily into the Jeep after her. She's nervous as a cat in the middle of Michigan Avenue rush hour. If this man suspects the two American nurses, it will be an easy enough thing to slit their throats from behind and drive off without a second thought.

Ginny leans over, pretending to fiddle with a few knobs and whispers, "Why did you give him morphine?"

"To knock him out. Our friend in the backseat has a tattoo of a snake under his watch. Didn't Cliff say one of the men in the desert had a snake tattoo?"

"What do we do until he falls asleep?" Ginny growls.

"You okay enough to show us around town a bit still?" Carlotta asks the man in the back.

At Monkaster's garbled attempt to talk, Carlotta turns. "Don't you worry, hon. We'll take good care of you." When she turns to face front, her face flickers with fury hot enough to scald. Ginny shivers. If she didn't know better, she'd think Carlotta was plotting murder.

10

Either Carlotta is a tremendous actress or she's fast asleep in the passenger seat, leaving Ginny yawning in the driver's seat and far too nervous to do much of anything useful. Carlotta directed Ginny around Cairo until Monkaster finally dropped off to sleep, then had Ginny stop at a nondescript building.

Carlotta leaped out of the car with an "I'll be back" before Ginny could quite figure out was happening.

A few minutes later, Carlotta popped out of the front door, carrying a box of who knows what and a coffee.

"For you," she'd said as she handed Ginny the confection in a cup.

Ginny had to hand it to Carlotta. She knew exactly what made everyone happy and had a knack for showing up exactly when she was needed.

Ginny is tired enough to fall asleep where she sits, but there's a German spy in her back seat, and now she's parked behind a broken-down military convoy.

They're maybe a ten-minute drive from the camp gate, and she's tempted to dump Monkaster on the side of the road and forget about trying to expose the spy ring. She could still hoof it home, right? But that's probably the stupidest thing she could do. Strike out in the desert at night. Alone.

She glances at her watch again. It's been at least two hours since Carlotta dosed Monkaster or whoever he is. She forces herself to stop jiggling her leg and waves at the GIs sitting by the side of the road. They look exhausted, and more than a few are wearing bandages.

With another quick glance into the backseat to assure herself that Monkaster truly is still sleeping, Ginny slides from the Jeep and trots to the last vehicle in line to see if she can help. An officer in a peaked crusher cap leans against the side of the Jeep, drawing on a cigarette and squinting at the wide expanse of blank sand.

At the sound of her approach, he turns, frowning at her from beneath a drooping mustache, and blows a rush of foul smoke in her direction.

Ginny ignores the insult. It isn't about her. Many officers resent babysitting the injured well behind enemy lines. Glancing at his shoulders for rank, she snaps a tidy salute. The gold oak leaf sparkles in the setting sun. Great. A major. They're stuck between captains who do the work and colonels who pull the strings, and they don't like being reminded that they still have to take orders.

She slaps on a glittering smile. "Lieutenant Lenarsic. I'm a nurse up at Huckstep. Is—"

"Unless you know how to change a tire, you can climb back into your Jeep and wait like the rest of us."

"Actually my father made sure I knew exactly how to change a tire. I've also put a man's intestines back into his body, sewn him up, and watched him return to the front a month later. I'll just check up the line to see if any of the men need some TLC." She gives the gaping man a finger wave and channels her best Carlotta impression, sashaying toward the troop carrier. Blast that ridiculous man. He probably hasn't even seen combat and is itching to jump in and throw men in front of machine guns.

"Ma'am?" A deep voice cuts into her thoughts, and Ginny smiles toward the host of eyes peering down at her.

"I'm a nurse at Huckstep. I don't have many supplies, but do any of you need anything I can help with?"

A second lieutenant helps Ginny into the carrier, and she makes her way down the row, checking bandages and talking with the men. None of these men is in dire need of medical attention. Something she is immensely grateful for as she jumps off the bumper.

"How far are we from the camp?" one of the boys calls.

"Not far. Someone's got a blown tire, I think. You should be on your way soon." No sooner has she said it than a squawk comes through the radio and the carrier's engine cranks over.

"See you up there soon, fellas." Ginny trots back past the major, throwing him a cheeky two-fingered salute before ducking into the Jeep to find Monkaster stirring and Carlotta still out cold. With shaking fingers, Ginny cranks over the engine and follows the cloud of dust, just far enough back that she can still somewhat see the road in front of her as she clicks on the Jeep's lights.

"What...?" Monkaster wipes at the drool hanging from the corner of his mouth.

"You passed out on the street," Ginny says, "and I have a shift starting in less than an hour. I couldn't leave you there, and I can't miss my shift, so I piled you into the backseat and headed back to the base. I hope you don't mind."

Monkaster yawns and stretches. "Not at all."

Ginny opens her mouth and closes it. She doesn't know what to say as they crawl down the road behind the slow-moving convoy.

Fortunately, Monkaster is sufficiently pompous to prattle about himself. Occasionally he slips in obviously probing questions that Ginny parries with the skill of an older sister hiding information from her little brother. In high school, no one ever did figure out where she went on Friday nights. Of course it was only to the roof for a bit of quiet, but who wanted Marcus chattering up there? As much as she loved him, he had a penchant for demanding to be right, even if he knew he was wrong.

She could use Marcus's pointed questions about now. Could use anyone as a buffer between herself and the cold watch of the man behind her. Shaking her keep herself awake, Ginny smiles at the man in the back seat and answers another question about troop movements and installations with some form of *What would a pretty little nurse like me know about a thing like that?* That he believes her act rather burns her butter, but she will see him twist for far worse offenses, and then what will he think?

A bare minute or two from the base, Ginny is done listening to his falsified exploits from throughout the war and asks, "So where are you from again?"

It's an innocent enough question, but his stiffening shoulders tell her she shouldn't have changed the subject so quickly. "Chicago, but I've been knocking around the world for a while. Why?"

"No reason really." Ginny raises a shoulder, cursing herself for having asked, just in case he turned the question on her.

"Where are you from?"

Blast. "Well, you'll never believe it, but I'm from Chicago too. But my guess is we don't run in the same circles. My dad's a pastor, and we live pretty close to the mission he works at. Inner city stuff."

"So you've learned to take care of yourself on the street?"

Ginny isn't sure how to navigate this minefield. She's pretended to be a bit of an airhead and not the street-smart kid Southside Chicago tends to produce. Just surviving the smell of the Union Stock Yards equips you to deal with most of life's hardships.

"You aren't who you're pretending to be, are you?" Monkaster leans back in his seat.

Ginny's mouth goes dry. Curse the darkness. She has no idea if he's mocking her, or telling her he likes her better without the getup, or is he hinting that he knows what she's doing. How she wishes she could see the man's shadowed face. "I—"

"If I may be bold, you are better off not trying to pretend. You are not suited."

Opting to assume he's still underestimating her, Ginny laughs, a hand touching the stone necklace at her throat. "You have to pretend in war, Mr. Monkaster. It's the only way to survive."

"Where did you get the beautiful pendant?" The man's voice has gone hard as granite.

The pendant has gone cold under her touch.

Ginny drops her hand to the steering wheel. "A friend gave it to me."

"A friend."

Her pendant is downright frigid, and Monkaster shifts like he's reaching for a gun. With barely a thought, Ginny yanks the wheel, letting the tire drop off the road and pop back on. The move serves to both throw Monkaster off balance and wake Carlotta. Ginny's never been so grateful to be following a convoy, but having the men not far in front of her won't stop Monkaster from shooting her in the back of the head.

"Sorry about that. I keep drifting off to sleep." Ginny's laugh is even more awkward than normal, knowing Monkaster likely isn't buying a word of it. "But the base is just around the corner." She nods at the barbed wire fencing curling along, pierced only occasionally by a guard tour.

Ginny's smile is tight, and she prays Carlotta has an idea of what to do with the man once they get to the base. Finally, blessedly, Ginny turns off the tarmac onto the crushed stone of the camp entrance and stops at the guard station. As the convoy disappears in the dark around the corner, Carlotta swings out of the car with an "I'll be back, sugar," and calls to one of the MPs, apparently named George.

With a great waving of Carlotta's hands, the two converse outside the guard hut. Ginny catches herself tapping her forefinger on the steering wheel and drops her hands into her lap. George switches on a flashlight and saunters to the Jeep. "Coming in later than expected, Lieutenant Lenarsic?"

"Ran into a civvy who needed some medical attention and then got caught behind the convoy."

George's light follows Ginny's over-the-shoulder gesture and captures Monkaster. The harsh beam flattens the fake journalist's features like a bad newspaper reproduction.

"No problem." George's smile is tight but obliging.

Does he know what's going on?

"Just need to pat you down, sir, and check your press credentials." The MP eases open the door.

With the last of her fraying control, Ginny springs out and saunters behind George and his gun, which leaves Monkaster no choice but to clamber from the vehicle.

"If you'll come this way, please."

At the MP's command, Monkaster glances at Carlotta in concern, but she gives wide, disarming smile, "We'll wait right here for you." The moment the guard shack door closes, Carlotta collapses against the Jeep's bumper. "For a minute there, I didn't think he'd fall for it. I told George to hold the idiot while I go find an officer."

"Please tell me you know a guy."

"Well, my guy is friends with an intelligence officer. I'll start with him."

They pile back into the Jeep and drive the vehicle to the motor pool. Carlotta trots off to find her latest squeeze, and Ginny sits for a moment listening to the whistling sound of the desert wind. Can it possibly be this easy to bring down a traitor?

Slipping from the driver's seat, Ginny yanks off her heels and trots back to the entrance. Just like the air, the sand is still scorching hot on her bare feet, but it reminds her of home—the Lake Michigan beaches in the height of August heat. If only the lake was here too.

She rounds the corner and stops cold. The door to the guard hut is wide open. The main room is empty and so is the one cell she can see. Heart pounding so hard her fingers ache with the pressure, Ginny turns, and there, between her and the rest of camp, stands a man, feet spread wide.

11

Ginny takes a tentative step backward. What's she supposed to do now? Just as she opens her mouth to scream, the man raises a wicked-looking gun. A Walther P38. A German-issued weapon.

"I wouldn't scream if I were you." He steps into the light of the guard hut, and she flinches. She'd expected Monkaster, but another man skims his tongue across his thin lips. She's seen him before but can't quite place—

His face ripples, and Ginny stumbles, a rock piercing her bare foot. Scrambling to stay upright, she scrounges her wits and squares her shoulders. For a moment, she'd seen another face—a slit-nosed viper. But that can't be right. Adrenaline must be making her hallucinate, right?

She squares her shoulders and lifts her chin. If someone had attacked the guard hut, the others would know. "What do you want?" Ginny manages to at least not sound terrified.

"You think I should pour my little villain's heart out to you? We're not in a motion picture. And there is no one coming to save you." The snake man, whoever he is, gestures for Ginny to enter the hut.

But she's not willing to cage herself in with this...this creature and shakes her head.

"None of your friends are who you thought. Even if they are still alive, none of them will get here in time to save you."

Ginny stiffens. Carlotta. "If you've done anything to—"

He grabs Ginny's arm, and she wheels on him, slamming the heel of her right hand into his nose, continuing the rotation to jam her left elbow into his gut.

Freedom. She takes half a step before he seizes her again, laughing even as blood pumps down his face.

A flicker of movement behind the man catches Ginny's eye. She snaps her attention back to the snake man, but it's a second too late. He saw hope on her face, even though she couldn't see what was moving in the gloom. He whirls around just as a shadow leaps from the darkness on the other side of the road. Ginny jerks free, just as the newcomer's curved dagger slashes toward the snake man's neck. But the snake man slashes out and catches hold of the other man's arm. The two men collide with a thud, grappling for the knife, twisting into the light. Ginny gasps.

Red hair and beard wild as a goat, Cliff grunts against the snake man's unearthly onslaught. "Cliff?" Ginny whispers. Cliff's face is sunken, exhausted, half-starved, but it's him. How?

Cliff slams the snake man's hand against the guardrail and grinds out, "Ginny, get help!"

Cliff's voice snaps Ginny from her frozen confusion, and she sprints to the hut, bursting through the doorway into complete chaos, like the khamsin raged through.

There's blood sprayed across the floor, dotting the piles of paper strewn everywhere. She turns, panic building, a movement shifts in the second, far cell, and she chokes back a scream

Monkaster sits in the cell, feet propped up. "Apophis is going to kill you." Gone is the fake, nebulous American accent, his words wrapped in jagged German clip. "Just like he killed the guard. And then he'll destroy the weak Allies, and there is no one to stop him."

Ginny doesn't answer as she completes a visual sweep, forcing herself to follow her dad's training. Assess the situation and then act. There has to be a radio somewhere.

"Cliff thought by taking me down, he'd stop what's coming. But no one can stop Apophis permanently."

She attacks a promising debris pile, throwing bits of paper everywhere until she unearths the box.

"The god Set can stop him for a night, but that's it. Stave off the inevitable for a moment. Is that what you want? To fight every day?"

She smashes the headset over her ears, clicks on the radio, and hears nothing. Not even the squeal of the radio trying to connect. She drops to her knees, feeling around the back of the radio, trying to make sense of the fragments of wire. Then she realizes...the entire innards of the radio are missing.

There's a shout outside, and she yanks off the headset.

"Oh dear." Monkaster is nearly giddy. "That doesn't sound good."

"Just shoot!" Cliff's voice is desperate.

Ginny flies out the door just as a gunshot explodes. At first, all she sees is Carlotta as she drops the gun and clatters backward, folding in on herself, weeping. Ginny snatches the gun from the ground and grabs hold of her friend who's clutching her bleeding hand. Had the gun backfired? Had she been shot?

"Where is the—" Ginny's pendant scorches blazing hot, and she screams, spinning. She can smell the burn of her skin. And the pendant suddenly goes cold. Ginny's hair stands on end, and she turns. The snake man stands holding...Cliff.

There's a glimmer of blood streaking Cliff's pale, drawn face, but he smiles grimly at Ginny. He's alive and depending on her...and the gun in her shaking hand, which has already backfired once.

"Do you think"—the snake man's tongue flickers across his lips—"that you, a mere human, can defeat me where the god Set only holds me at bay?"

And that's when Ginny realizes why the woman didn't want her to leave. Monkaster is nothing but a pawn. "You're Apophis." She can hear the terror in her voice.

The snake man leers. "Human brains are so"—he licks his lips again and taps Cliff's skull—"tiny."

Ginny takes a step back and bumps into Carlotta, who wraps an arm around her friend. Ginny thinks of the Bedouin woman again. The reason she contacted Ginny. *"Aset holds the strongest magic, and we might do together what I cannot do alone."* Ginny is far from alone. She steadies her stance. She doesn't want to risk hitting Cliff, but she is a good shot, especially at this range. The pendant warms, giving off a soft glow.

Apophis's attention drops to the pendant, and his sneer slips a fraction.

"Perhaps we're more powerful than you think." Carlotta nods to the shadows behind Apophis.

The darkness glimmers, shifting, condensing into the shape of the Bedouin woman. She's carrying a wicked spear, and the sands swirl under her feet.

"Ah the human ward of Set," Apophis sneers. "We now have a complete assortment. We also have Horus." He nods at Cliff. "The wise little Thoth." He nods at Carlotta. "And little Aset's ward now too."

Ginny's mind is scrambling. What is happening? Did he mean that she is Aset?

Apophis laughs, the margins of the sound slipping into a hiss. "So much work and planning, Thoth. And yet, you will fail to erase me as you do every night."

Carlotta growls, and Apophis lifts the gun to Cliff's temple in reminder of the stakes.

"Take the shot, Ginny." Cliff sounds far too calm.

No. No. No. The word repeats in Ginny's head.

"Salma," Cliff says to the Bedouin woman, "you have my permission."

Apophis's grin is wicked. "I wonder if, without Horus, your plan will work?"

Cliff looks Ginny in the eye and gives a reassuring nod. She shakes her head, pleading with him not to do whatever it is he's thinking. He smiles, closes his eyes, and drops down, giving a hair's breadth of an opening. Ginny takes the shot at the same moment the Bedouin woman throws her spear.

Both bullet and spear thudding home. The snake man's smile fades, flickering between human and snake before finally sinking, dwindling, folding in on itself, flaking away into sand.

Silence stretches.

Ginny blinks, not quite believing what she just witnessed.

Beside the shifting mound of sand, Cliff rolls onto his back with a sickening groan.

"Cliff?" Ginny's gun drops to the ground with a cold thud. She stumbles forward, the pull of her love dragging her down, down, down until she's holding his pale face in her hands as he sucks in air, gasping. Her hands release his face, and she's shouting orders to orderlies and fellow nurses who aren't there as she tears open his shirt. Blood bubbles with leaking air. His lungs straining.

No, no, no. She presses her hand over the gaping knife wound, and Cliff scrabbles to capture her hand in his. His mouth lifts in a broken smile. "You will..." He sips an inhale and starts again. "You will always have me."

The next inhale, he winces, and Ginny's hold on his hands tightens as if she can single-handedly keep him here. "Don't you dare leave me like this, Clifford Raymond Floyd. Don't you dare." Her voice cracks.

Cliff's eyes flicker open and catch Ginny's. "...love you."

She smooths her hand over the deep crevices carved into Cliff's forehead. "I will love you forever, Cliff."

He smiles up at her, blinks once, and then he droops, his arm dropping lifeless.

Ginny rocks back on her heels, her soul drifting into the ground even as his flies.

Carlotta kneels across from Ginny, her hand smoothing down Cliff's eyelids and closing his shirt. "I told him he wasn't ready yet. That he wasn't strong enough."

Ginny gapes at her friend. "What are you talking about?"

Carlotta sighs, pushes to her feet, holding the discarded gun, and points at the blowing pile of sand remains. "It wasn't just about spies. It was about finding Apophis and destroying him."

"And we have." The Bedouin woman steps from the shadows. She kicks the mound of sand so it scatters, mixing with the desert, the remaining sparks diluting, weakening, until Ginny could no longer tell natural sand from the remains of Apophis.

The Bedouin woman picks up her spear and looks down at Cliff.

Ginny leaps to her feet, frustration, confusion, and anger boiling into a venomous concoction. "You! You did this."

"No." Her single, gentle word is filled with regret. "My life and the lives of others aren't mine to defend or destroy. I am cursed to fulfill my assignment so that I can return home and live out the life I've seen, even if it may kill me to do so. It was my duty to work with you to dispose of Apophis, and I have done so. The flyer was told to stand down and chose not to."

"Why?" Ginny sobs. "Why not?"

Carlotta eases a knowing arm around her friend's shoulder.

And Ginny realizes. "Me. He came because of me."

Ginny's stomach rebels, and she flings herself away from her friend just in time to lose what little she'd eaten. She watches the bile leech into the ground, and lets her head hang, pleading with the earth to swallow her too. Cliff had been alive all this time. "Did you know?" She stands, hands clenched at her sides as she faces her friend.

"Yes," Carlotta whispers. "We thought we were protecting him. Argus and I, we thought—"

Voices lift from the base, and the Bedouin woman's eyes narrow. Her body flickers a moment before dissipating into shadow.

"Are you just going to let her go?"

Carlotta gives a rough laugh. "You think I could stop Set's agent from leaving?"

A herd of MPs storms around the corner and comes to a screeching halt at the sight of Ginny covered in blood, Carlotta clutching a gun, and Cliff's lifeless body.

♀

THE MPS HAD TAKEN Ginny's meandering statement and then Carlotta's, before chalking Ginny's bizarre tale up to grief and shock. But with the mysterious snake man was gone and the capture of Monkaster, Ginny knows the Apophis ring will fall.

As she leaves the hut, Ginny hears a few of the officers whispering in the corner. Lieutenant Colonel Ames is missing. Ginny stumbles to a stop. The reason snake man had looked so familiar is that he was Worthington and Showboat's father. Monkaster had happily given up Showboat, who was caught red-handed trying to burn paperwork he'd stolen.

The theory is that father and son had taken Worthington's death hard and welcomed the German spy with open arms. And if the whispers were true, something darker still.

The officers are sure they'll never find the elder Ames. Ginny knows they're right, but not for the reasons they think. Or at least she's pretty sure they're right. In the blazing light of day, Ginny isn't sure what she saw, but when the doctor suggested a psych eval, she stopped trying to convince anyone.

It's been forty-eight hours or so since she lost Cliff. Again. Finally free, Ginny wanders back to her tent in the gathering dark. Her feet slide in the windblown sand covering the walkways, and she slogs down the uneven path, carefully watching where she places her feet. The last thing she needs is a sprained ankle.

All she wants to do now is go home, hug her folks and little brother, and hunker down for a month or ten. There's nothing tying her to this place anymore. Cliff is really and truly gone. Maybe it's time to let others take up the fight.

She turns into the row of tents and stops. It smells like...smoke? Jerking her chin up, Ginny realizes that there's a flicker of fire outside her tent. Slipping the knife from her belt, she bolts down the pathway, shouting, cursing, angry that the world is still dumping on her.

No one is outside her tent tending the fire. Ginny slumps, frowning at the coals, which don't seem to be consuming the kindling. She squats and uses her knife to poke at the sticks. They topple and send sparks floating into the night air.

"Careful," a voice emerges from the tent doorway, and Ginny leaps to her feet. The Bedouin woman is hovering there, the package she'd first brought outstretched. "You might want to burn this before you snuff that."

"Why in the name of everything that's holy would I want to burn

Cliff's journals?" Ginny seizes the bundle and clutches it to her chest, protecting it from the strange creature in her midst. She's still not sure if the woman is friend or foe.

The woman shrugs and squats comfortably, assuming the air of a storyteller. "Do you want them to think you are crazy or that he was? He was a good man. The men of shadow would twist the words there until they cut you and him. Better to give them nothing."

Ginny knows she's right. The end of the journal makes Cliff sound like he'd lost his mind in the desert. "I could just cut those pages out."

"And have them ask where you found the journal and where the missing pages are?"

Ginny rubs a thumb across the spine, feeling for the places Cliff must have touched. "But they're evidence." It's obvious even to Ginny that the argument lacks merit. With the information Carlotta and Ginny already have and Showboat's testimony, the intelligence branch can investigate. Cliff's journal doesn't have any more information. In fact, if MI6 or the OSS sees it, they might dismiss everything else as the raving fancy of a grieving woman and a sunstruck man.

"Words can be shackles as much as they can set us free." The woman's eyes flicker red from the flames. "Sometimes destruction is the way, and sometimes not. Today, you must choose." She groans to her feet. "I have done what I could to destroy Apophis. The one you call Cliff was a worthy adversary and ally. I would see him rest in peace if I could. You have the power of Aset to choose how you keep him alive—in chaos or peace."

She nods once, waves her hand over the flame in an odd sign of blessing, bows, then floats away. As she turns the corner, her black robes flicker, and the shadow of a fork-tailed dog trots down the path.

"Grief does strange things to people," Ginny tells herself. Surely she doesn't believe the woman is an agent of Set or that Apophis is anything other than a ring of spies. There is no larger-than-life snake trying to devour the world, right? The fire crackles, snapping at her feet. Ginny's surprised to see that the kindling is curling now, burning. If she's going to destroy the journal, she must do it now, before Carlotta comes for her.

She still has no idea what Carlotta does or doesn't know or who she really is. There's so much about war that is strange, including the depth of friendships made in such a short time and with so little real knowledge of one another.

Ginny lifts the journal to her lips, lingering a moment to smell the leather tinged with a bit of gasoline. Cliff's smell. She loosens her grip on the bundle, letting it tumble into the flames. The fire flares, gobbling the pages in a greedy rush. And then with a quiet puff, the fire falls in on itself and crumbles into the sand. A small scorch mark is the only sign there had been a fire. Ginny kneels, hesitantly touching the cool earth.

"You okay?"

At Carlotta's voice, Ginny whirls, scattering red sand like fairy dust.

"The journals are gone." Ginny's voice sounds hollow, like she's in a dream or maybe just waking from one. There had been a journal, right? And a woman? Suddenly, she's not so sure.

"Oh honey, I'm sorry." Carlotta pulls Ginny's tall, sturdy frame down into a fierce hug. "What happened?"

"I don't know? I think...that woman." Ginny stares off to where she'd seen the shadow of the dog disappear.

Carlotta releases Ginny and swings around to search the same vicinity as her friend, like their combined examination might reveal new information. "The Bedouin?"

"How did you know her?"

"Oh, honey. It's a long story. Sometimes when you need something, you make deals you regret later. But without all the pieces, even the chaos, we could never have brought justice. I hope one day you'll see that."

"Was it real? I mean all the..." Ginny is terrified of voicing what her mind can't make sense of.

"What do you think?" Carlotta taps the pendant on Ginny's collarbone.

It isn't an answer, but Ginny's too tired to push. What does it matter now anyway?

Carlotta opens the door to their bunk and waves Ginny through. "Since the colonel was involved, the Brits are taking over the investigation."

Ginny nods numbly. That's a good thing isn't it? Someone on the outside who will be unbiased, objective. They'll see Cliff's actions as heroic, not crazy.

Somewhere beyond the perimeter, a woman's laughter merges with the howl of some creature. Next to Ginny, Carlotta shivers and loops her arm around Ginny's waist.

"Do me a favor?" Ginny follows her friend into the tent. "Don't tell them about the weird things at the end of the journal. No one back home needs to think he went crazy in the end. Let them think he was capable and calm, dying in the desert from a plane crash."

"God of the sky to the end," Carlotta agrees. "The desert will remember him, even if no one else does. The war will end, but this place won't let us go, Ginny. Don't ever doubt that."

♀

ABOVE THEM, a falcon shuffles his wings, acknowledging that the god of chaos had proven helpful...this time.

AUTHOR'S NOTE

Thank you for hanging out with me for a quick jaunt into WWII. If you know anything about me, you'll know that I am a proud geek who nerds out about history, science, and books...and I also cut my teeth on fantasy and myth. So why not combine crazy historical facts with a little flair of myth and fantasy?

My history buffs out there are likely wondering how much of this story is real and how much of it is my weird imagination. I am so glad you asked.

First, before anyone drops me an email, the plane on the cover is not a Warhawk. It's simply the only WWII-looking plane I could find to fit the cover. The Warhawk is a single-engine plane.

But Johannes Eppler, alias Peter Monkaster, was a real German spy. He and an accomplice infiltrated Allied confidences by posing as American reporters—sometimes described as a wire service correspondent or stringer working for outlets back in the US. The pair frequented popular haunts in Cairo—Groppi's, Shepheard's Hotel, Kit-Kat Club—posing as ordinary expats enjoying the city. They were supposed to pass along information on Allied troop strength, supply movements, and morale to Rommel's Afrika Korps. Through local informants, questions from US servicemen, counterfeit banknotes, and the discovery of a faulty radio transmitter, MI6 agents eventually dug into Eppler's false press credentials and uncovered the plot. Of course the mythological Set, Aset, Thoth and Horus were not part of the real history. But who knows that a pair of nurses wasn't involved in tipping off the MI6 agents?

I did change the name of the spy organization from *Operation Salaam* to *Apophis* to give the reader a question as to who, in the story, might really be running the show. One of the Egyptian myths that shows the need for the god of chaos is the story of Set fighting the colossal serpent who tries to devour Ra's boat (the sun) and lurks in the desert waiting to ambush unsuspecting people and gods. Set is one of the few gods powerful enough to defeat Apophis.

Of course that doesn't prevent the rest of the pantheon, including the falcon god, Horus, from truly hating Set. Make of that tie what you will. But I am a firm believer in finding beauty in hard things.

Camp Huckstep was a real place and housed the enormous 38th General Hospital. The camp still exists as an Egyptian base. The ferrying of P-40s through the Crescent Loop (from Cairo to the China-Burma-India theater) was also real, as is the route I depicted through Africa. The Nubian desert where Cliff went down was the most dangerous leg because of the frequent sandstorms, which occur the most in April—also the month when that part of the story takes place.

All of the characters except those mentioned above are figments of my imagination...and a savvy reader will notice ties to the other books in the Threads of the Lost Myth series. I won't spoil the fun, but you can drop me an email to see if you're right (janyre@janyretromp.com).

You're also likely to notice nods to the famous Silver Screen movie *Casablanca.* Not only in the atmosphere, dialogue winks, and themes of betrayal and love versus duty but also in some morally gray decisions. Conflict is almost never as black and white as we'd like it to be, and sometimes we're forced to choose between equally good or bad decisions rather than clear right or wrong. My goal is to at least listen to the people who have different opinions from mine and be open to choosing something other than my own preference.

And my family will tell you I don't have this ignoring-my-own-preferences thing down...which leads me to my prayer that, at the very least, I won't make decisions I can never take back.

If you're interested in learning more about Camp Huckstep or the 38th General Hospital, you can check out some declassified documents here: https://www.cia.gov/readingroom/docs/CIA-RDP78T05439A000400380066-8.pdf and Army archives here: https://achh.army.mil/history/book-wwii-medsvcsinmedtrnmnrthrtrs-chapter2.

For Egyptian mythology, I recommend *The Complete Gods and Goddesses of Ancient Egypt* by Richard H. Wilkinson or, if you want a narrative style retelling, try Roger Lancelyn Green's *Tales of Ancient Egypt.*

And don't miss the recipes for the desserts mentioned. They're at the very back of the book.

If you enjoyed this story, I'd love for you to:

1. Post a review at any of the major booksellers. Even a sentence helps other readers find my books.
2. Check out the rest of the Threads of the Lost Myth Series. Where each book finds another thread of the lost myth tangled in history's secrets.

OTHER BOOKS IN THE THREADS OF THE LOST MYTH SERIES

Grab the rest of the series where:

History remembers. Myth echoes. The truth lies between—

and every era weaves another fragment of the thread.

☥

The Scorpion Thief (coming April 2026)

A cursed artifact.

A deadly Cold War game.

Two estranged sisters—one guardian, one thief—collide as Tut's treasures are readied for an American tour. From Cairo's streets to New Orleans's bayous, political intrigue, family betrayal, and myth entwine in a haunting thriller. "Perfect for fans of Kate Morton, Sarah Penner, and the classic movie *The Maltese Falcon*." ~Julie Cantrell, *New York Times* bestselling author of *Into the Free*

Available wherever books are sold.

Find purchase links here:

https://beautifuluglyme.com/my-writing/the-scorpion-thief/

☥

Burning the Raven Tree (coming September 2026)

A survivor accused of a decade-old murder.

A disgraced lawyer with everything to prove.

And an ancient oak that has borne witness for a millennium.

In 1960s northern Michigan, a town is haunted by legend whispers of the raven witch and child killer. But when Marcus Lenarsic arrives, he finds not a monster but a broken woman bound by secrets. *Burning the Raven Tree* is a gothic historical thriller teaming with ghosts, justice, and memory—perfect for fans of Kate Morton, Simone St. James, William Kent Krueger, and the classic film *Rebecca*.

Preorder here: https://amzn.to/3KBgKyo

⚲

Oracle of the Silent City (coming March 2027)

A basement prison.

A city ruled by shadows.

And a family hunted by Jimmy Hoffa's men as a wicked storm bears down.

Detroit, 1962. Beneath the roar of factories and the pulse of union power, the city smolders—an underworld ruled by men who think they're gods. When a woman holding the oracle's truth vanishes, her scarred brother-in-law must descend into the depths before Hoffa's men close in. *Oracle of the Silent City* is a myth-infused gothic thriller of loyalty, corruption, and ghosts that won't stay buried—perfect for fans of Simone St. James, *Shawshank Redemption*, and the classic movie *The Godfather*.

⚲

Every story leaves a lingering echo... and the next chapter is already calling. Continue the journey with a first look at the opening of first myth-infused tale in the series, where old secrets stir and fate begins to shift.

THE SCORPION THIEF (SAMPLE)

Chapter I

July 20, 1976

When the woman strolls by the Cairo Museum right in front of Noura Marquette, cool as a cucumber despite the heat, Noura is certain she's mistaken. The last time she saw her younger sister, Estelle was storming out of their father's Tel Aviv apartment, spouting a not-so-subtle curse on Noura and her descendants, all sealed with the tiny bloody handprint smeared across Estelle's back.

As the lithe woman passes into a building's shadow, Noura's mind tangles in opposing desires to dart after the woman and to simply walk away as her sister had. And so she stands like some tragic statue, trembling, useless, unable to do anything as usual.

Estelle's twin emerges to sunlight slashing across her scarred arm, the languid sway of her hip. Petulant laughter lifts from the woman. So familiar she might have crawled from the twisted mire of the past. Noura shakes free of the image.

It's ridiculous. There is no way Estelle happens to be in Cairo at the same moment as her older sister.

Would Estelle want to blow Egypt to smithereens for killing their brother? Perhaps. But walk the streets laughing? Not a chance.

Taking a step away from the apparition is like slogging through quicksand. Yet Noura drags one foot and then another toward the museum steps, the basket on her head tottering with each step so that she has to steady it with a hand. She is nearly free from the blasted biological pull when she realizes what she's just thought.

Noura spins, fingers sparking from the slam of adrenaline. Blow Egypt to smithereens? Knowing Estelle's associates, bombs are indeed a possibility.

"Dr. Marquette?" Dr. Christine Lilyquist's call from the museum archway is muddy with concern. Noura winces. Here she is, dithering about on the street when she would normally be inside the museum already working.

"Coming," Noura answers her mentor, still half-facing the woman curving onto Merit Basha. Noura shades her eyes with a hand. The slope of the woman's nose isn't right. And she has a strand of dark hair escaping her scarf, not blond, right? And so thin. Noura can't help worrying about her sister...the woman...whoever she is.

The apparition disappears around the salmon pink museum building, and everything falls into its proper place—a street full of strangers. Noura steadies the basket and mentally stuffs the messy ache for her sister down with the rest of her childhood memories, and then bricks up that part of her soul. After all, you can't hurt stone.

"Are you all right?" The sun shimmers behind Dr. Lilyquist, turning her hair into a halo of gold. Appropriate since the Met's lead Egyptologist is a near goddess in their field.

"Thought I saw someone I knew." Noura slams down the last mental brick.

"Someone I should know?" Dr. Lilyquist squints into the crowd.

"An old classmate."

The half-truth snaps Dr. Lilyquist from her search. While Noura's father worked at the American embassy, he was a lowly librarian. Which means ferreting out an old classmate, who wouldn't have access to funding or influence, isn't worth the effort.

Noura smiles, exuding all that is harmonious. Her practiced submission is enough to make Dr. Lilyquist nod and then stride through the museum doors. Noura's shoulders relax the tiniest bit. Dr. Lilyquist knows little of the festering trouble Noura's siblings caused. If she had any idea, she might never allow Noura near the artifacts of King Tutankhamun's tomb destined to tour the US. Noura's career would be dead before it came to life.

As the pair ducks under the doorway's keystone sculpture of Aset, Noura can't help but think of how the Egyptian goddess resurrected her slain husband. Powerful, unrepentant, and able to battle death itself. What Noura wouldn't do for such power.

Dr. Lilyquist trots down the few stairs into the sunken display area and strides between the sarcophagi, leaving Noura to scramble along in her mentor's footsteps. They pass one after another of Egyptian royalty laid out in mind-numbing repetition. But as she passes the statue of the falcon-headed Horus, she shivers, feeling like he's watching her, spreading his wings over her in request to help him repeat the miracle his mother, Aset, had made possible. Not that Noura would ever consider raising the dead. After all, the only thing Aset accomplished was a rivalry between her son and Set, the god of chaos. That battle has Egyptians to this day shrugging at tragedy and citing the necessity to balance chaos and peace—the *isfet* of Set and the *ma'at* of Horus. Only Anubis and Osiris can judge in the afterlife.

Apparently life thinks Noura needs her peace balanced out. Even the thought of her chaotic sister has Noura's attention skittering sideways. Their father would laugh at the preposterous thought of gods or fate.

A pulse of anxiety zings down Noura's arms, almost as if Father is standing before her, his sharp expression saying more than his caustic words ever did.

But Father is not here. And as Dr. Lilyquist trots up the back stairs, Noura shoves his accusations in with the walled-off detritus of the past. She braces her basket and scrambles to the second floor. Here, the items from King Tutankhamun's tomb are displayed, or rather, scattered about in horror-filling disarray. Noura itches to reorganize. She knows her place, however, and would never offend her Egyptian counterparts by presuming to know better.

Fortunately for her sanity, the American team's area is more organized. In the front room, Noura slips past precise mountains of foam sheets and various archival packing materials. Behind the piles, John and Abel lift their utility knives in greeting and return to measuring and cutting with focused, if slightly jocular, impunity. If Noura didn't know better, she would think the British packing duo were high-performing toddlers bent on world domination. In reality, they've packed Tut's treasures before and are an invaluable resource for the Americans—both for their packing skills and for their knowledge of their Egyptian coworkers.

Noura ducks through an archway into the back alcove. At a table near the far wall, the two conservators, Frank Caddel and Theodore Fabre, bend over one of the three-thousand-year-old objects, painstakingly repairing a crack in the ancient blue paint made from ground glass. Theo glances up from his work with a roguish wink, and Noura, who has lifted shy fingers in happy response, snatches her blasted fingers down, praying Dr. Lilyquist didn't notice either the wink or Noura's stupid flushed cheeks.

A quick glance tells Noura her mentor is blessedly ignorant as she strides out the door, frowning over a document.

Noura stomps out the interest flickering in her middle and paces to her tiny desk wedged into the front corner. Theo may be a talented conservationist with a droll sense of humor and a dogged willingness to help her rifle through the souks for the only type of pencil Mr. Caddel will use, but Noura doesn't have a permanent job in the Egyptology department at the Met. And she will not get sacked for flights of romantic fantasy. Professional women don't have the luxury of appearing weak. And that includes becoming involved with the opposite sex.

Theo's sparkling brown eyes included.

Noura deposits the basket of provisions onto the floor, unwraps the dull brown scarf from her hair, then sets the supplies on a shelf and the bag of food out of the way of the antiquities. The team will nibble at the snacks until they can take a dinner break well after dark.

For now, she unearths her notebook from under the neat stack of fifty-five card files. One file for every artifact Dr. Lilyquist and the Met's director selected for the tour to the US.

When Noura ducks into the alcove to assess where the others are on today's duties, she realizes what the conservators are working on—the necklace with the vulture pendant. Acrid panic explodes through her at how far behind they are.

Noura taps her leg in a semi-useless attempt to scrape away the corrosion eating her muscles. "Still working on the pendant?" She is pleased to hear the complete absence of bite in her tone.

"It needed more repair than we expected." Mr. Caddel doesn't even look up. "And Hoving is on a mission."

Thomas Hoving is the brilliant Metropolitan Museum of Art director with a shifting wish list that sometimes leaves everyone on his team without solid foothold. Noura crosses her ankles and leans a nonchalant hip against the table, but she still has a death grip on the notebook clutched to her chest. "I'm afraid to ask."

"He wants Selket," Theo says.

"Is that all?" Noura laughs. "The Egyptians will never let us have her." They'd consider it a sacrilege to dismantle the chest containing Tutankhamun's organs.

"And yet, Mr. Hoving won't leave without the statue."

Theo is right. The team will be tasked with the impossible.

Feet, Noura thinks, meet the cliff over which your career will plummet.

"It's your fault, you know." Mr. Caddel adjusts his reading glasses so he can glare at her in full 20/20 vision.

"My fault?" If only her notebook could ward off Mr. Caddel's evil eye.

"Ignore him." Theo positions his brush in its holder and rests his forearms on the worktable. "You made a brilliant observation. Frank's peeved because he didn't notice that the goddess was pegged onto the canopic chest rather than carved from one piece."

"It was obvious in the photos from when they discovered the tomb," Noura says. "I've studied those 1920 photos a million times."

"Still," Mr. Caddel grumbles into his paint pot, "you're the one who went gaga over the scorpion goddess and convinced Hoving to add her."

"And it'll be a better show because of it." Theo gives his fellow conservator a nudge and picks up his brush again, cutting off the discussion. "We'll be finished soon, and the leopard head won't take long."

Unfortunately, Theo's support doesn't stop Noura's thoughts from tumbling. First, she never convinced Mr. Hoving to do anything. And second, she understands both Mr. Caddel's concern and Mr. Hoving's desire. Selket is compelling, as is the scorpion perched on her linen headscarf. With her long neck curved so she stares over her shoulder, you can practically hear her dare you to take what isn't yours. She is the goddess with a scorpion's power over snakes, who guards the pharaoh, who paralyzes and tightens the throat. She is both the goddess of death and the goddess of healing.

Noura walks the perimeter of the back room. Changing the list now, while Hoving's prerogative, makes the weight of history and responsibility press heavier. Endless checklists and traipsing through the crowded market aren't what Noura had in mind while capering through art history and museum curating classes. The goal of the actual exhibit —with the clamor of excitement and lines of captivated people—seems a marathon away...and she has never run for anything but danger in her entire life.

Noura makes a note in her notebook and grimaces as her fingers leave wet marks on the page. Under the stress of the show and heat of construction lights she scrounged from the market, she's now sweating enough to make anyone think she's run that marathon. She flutters the front of her linen shirt, wishing for more than the small reprieve.

"Think New York January cold," Theo says with a sardonic backhand to his voice.

Noura bites her lip to keep in the snort of laughter. She's not certain if he's talking to her or himself or Mr. Caddel, who has yet to stop grumbling under his breath. Though Mr. Caddel's temper is as hot and unpredictable as the stereotypical red-headed Bostonian he is, Theo can rib his friend into better humor.

"Snowmen?" Theo's voice soars louder to trail her across the room. "Skiing? Icicles?"

"New York can keep its January cold." The rejoinder leaves Noura's lips before she remembers her resolve. No relationships. She is stone. She flees through the archway. There will be no sparkling eyes for her.

"How about ice cream?" Noura hears a scraping of wood upon wood and turns to see Theo standing. He meanders toward her and raises an eyebrow. He is definitely asking her.

His sloppy grin and tapping of his fingers against his leg have her heart screaming *yes!* How do you say no to such reckless adorableness?

"If I remember," he says in a voice low enough only she hears, "you love mango ice."

And she does. Heaven knows she does. What she wants crashes into the reality of her position, and the riptide drags her into a murky pool. "I...that is—"

"We have work to do, gentlemen." John's staid voice saves Noura from replying.

Turning her back to the conservators, Noura hides her flaming cheeks by peering over the molds John and his coworker are assembling. If she didn't know better, she would believe they're a madman's three-dimensional puzzle tumbled into foam boxes. John numbers a knob of foam, then marks the bit on a schematic of the crate. The two British men have a method to their madness. Behind her, she hears Theo walking back to his station.

"If those two stop complaining about the temperature long enough to finish," John says, "we will be ready for the piece."

"We'll need photos of the repairs before we pack it."

From John's bored nod at Noura's reminder, he's far less ruffled than she is to be in Egypt, packing ancient burial treasures. She covers her faux pas by checking the stock of packing material and then frowning, making sure to note absolutely nothing on her pad of paper.

Like a novice oaf, she can't quite believe she, or any of the American team, is in Cairo. The tour of King Tut's artifacts is not just a feat of archaeological magic. It is a political sleight of hand as well. Until a few months ago, Egypt was on the US's "strained relations" list. And yet, here they are, using the tour to court the country that murdered Noura's brother.

The memory of bombs jars the marrow of her bones. Muscles aching as they strained to keep her body from flying into a million frantic pieces. Estelle's whimper from a needle stick, the slam of the door behind Maman, and Noura's attempt to finish homework under the barrage. And all of that before the final war.

Noura grips the edge of the foam container and sucks in air, inhaling, desperate to extinguish the firestorm erupting in her chest.

"Are you quite all right, Dr. Marquette?" John says from too close behind her.

"Of course."

His bushy gray brows squish together, simultaneously telling Noura that he sees her lie, and he feels obligated to protect her. It's a kind, fatherly gesture that can destroy her career in a smothering, dismissive concern for her suitability.

"Do you need anything?" Noura's words are over-bright as she ushers the bumbling hero away from her carefully constructed walls.

John's attention slides from her to the others, pondering their huddled conversation, and then back in decision. "Provided you've brought a decent goat cheese, I'm right as rain."

Noura wipes the relief from her face and then drops her hand, tranquil, to her side. "I have your favorite."

"You never fail to amaze me," he says. "Though I shouldn't be surprised. You conjured construction lights that didn't cost the entire budget. Of course you found dill-spiked cheese."

From John, a fellow expert in the art of market negotiation, this is high praise, and Noura grins her thanks.

"Hooray for the best vittles this side of the Nile," Mr. Caddel shouts from the other room, as if she's only good for grocery shopping.

Noura bites off the urge to put the pejorative-slinging man in his place and instead smiles at John. "You'll have the crate ready by tonight?"

"Of course."

The waving hand of Mr. Caddel beckons Noura toward his station on the far side of the long room. "We're nearly out of polyvinyl acetate." Mr. Caddel nods to the bowl of glue-like paint.

Noura flips through her list. "The hotel courier should have brought it this morning."

Mr. Caddel frowns and glances out the door like he wonders if he should report her incompetence.

In a country that moves with the speed of careful respect, it will take time to track down the delivery. And the list of today's tasks is longer than the Mississippi River. "Do you have enough for today?"

"Maybe." Mr. Caddel tips the pot toward Theo.

Noura can't read the silent communication flying between the two men, but Theo grinds to his feet. Apparently she and Theo are going to locate the paint now.

"I'm headed to the hotel for a shipment." She tells the disinterested room before grabbing her bag. "Try to get the leopard head's condition report started before the end of the night."

Theo's already holding the door for her, his tie askew under his five o'clock shadow. Noura resists the urge to straighten the silk and instead trundles into the museum proper.

Noura can almost hear her sister grumble about Noura hiding away behind a rambling walk and her meek hesitations. Why can't Noura straighten a handsome man's tie and flirt a little? Loosen up. But then Estelle, who was the American-blond-bombshell type made famous by Marilyn Monroe, never followed the rules and got away with her demands because everyone, including Noura, bent around her.

Until Noura couldn't anymore.

The fact that Noura is in Cairo is proof she isn't who she used to be. So maybe Noura can flirt a little. Especially with the one coworker who seems to view her as both a desirable woman and a talented curator.

As Theo opens the door to the street, Noura does her best to sashay up the steps, where she slips her hand into the curve of his elbow. Her fingers tingle at the strength in his biceps, and her knees shake at her audacity. To her delight, he rewards Noura's boldness with a golden grin —the sun god, Ra, as he wakes for the morning—and no one could miss Theo's little hop-skip as they stroll from the building. His tailored suit and square jaw scream that he's far too mature for his goofy nature and the wild crook in his nose. There's a story behind the dichotomy that tempts her curiosity enough to distract from her normal catastrophizing about everything.

The Nile Hilton, where the paint should be, is across the street and down a smidgen. Noura forces herself to match Theo's unhurried steps, even when he stops to pluck a tiny rose from a bush in the front garden. Somehow, despite how warm she is already, her neck flushes further.

"Do you mind diverting a bit?" Theo twirls the delicate pink blossom in his fingers as he plucks the thorns from the slender stem. His lashes bow, penitent, across his cheek.

"Oh, I don't mind." Noura's voice is as soft as she imagines the petals are. It's the answer the world expects of her. She truly doesn't mind the momentary reprieve from the stifling room and harried preparations... as long as this side trip isn't held against her.

"Good." He toys with the flower until she tears her attention from the safety of the rose to the man standing a breath away.

"Noura." Her name sounds long and round in his mouth. Theo waits, seeking permission, something few have ever done for her.

She swallows, vainly searching for her professionalism.

At some unbidden signal from her, his knuckles coax back the edge of Noura's headscarf, and he slips the rose behind her ear. Her entire soul is now nestled obediently in the man's palm.

"A beautiful flower for a beautiful woman," he says, and she stiffens as the words circle, a writhing snake of memories plucking her from her comfortable nest and plunging her back two decades.

Noura's father, talking to Maman. When they'd been happy. Before a pale-faced Maman almost evaporated, and Grandmere swept her away. Noura shakes her head, dragging herself from the labyrinthine memory. It's a common enough sentiment.

"Thank you." She touches the edges of the fragile flower, reminding herself that she, like a rose, is not without protection.

Theo's brows curve in quizzical confusion.

"Sorry," Noura says, scrambling for explanation. "Got pricked."

His expression clouds.

"From a thorn?" Her voice lifts stupidly, like she's asking his permission to lie.

He doesn't seem to catch the odd tone and holds his elbow out for her. His lips slide into a hopeful quirk, and she's stunned to realize that this hardworking, cheeky man is nervous. She makes him nervous. The idea unbends her, and she shakes off the tentacles of the past and the relentless crush of the onrushing future.

By the time Theo purchases a mango ice for her and they wander toward the hotel, the sun reclines below the roofline. Though Noura is exhausted, Theo's puppy enthusiasm makes her forget herself for the first time in years. As they arrive at the hotel steps, she bats her eyelashes as Grandmere demanded she do for Charles. In contrast to her ex-fiancé's laughing response to the one time she tried, Theo's crooked smile blooms in response.

Theo opens the door for her, and they whisk into the hotel reception, full of expected success.

"I am sorry, miss." The desk clerk twists his hands. "The delivery was sent this morning. Perhaps you misplaced it?"

"I didn't misplace it." She grits her teeth as the entire charade crumbles under the earthquake of understanding. It's one thing to use unfortunate events to court her or even to contrive for time alone, but quite another to lie and make her look like an incompetent fool who can't keep a delivery schedule straight.

Noura bows to the clerk, then spins on her heel, striding through the lobby and out the doors before launching into Theo. "Why did you let me ask for the paint when you knew it was already at the museum?" The nerve of the scheming man. Charles was right. She's a romantic fool.

"I didn't...that is..." Theo extends his hands in entreaty, brows pinched together.

She backs out of his reach, hating the impotent shake in her arms and the churning sound of tears and anger in her voice, and despising her confounded heart for hoping that her mind is wrong.

"I didn't..." Theo sucks in a breath, considering.

Again. Noura let herself be fooled again. "But you guessed."

At the inclination of his head, Noura stalks across the street. Perhaps she was wrong about Maman's selfishness. Maybe she abandoned them because Father belittled Maman's intelligence one too many times. Theo dogs her footsteps, but Noura's determined to arrive first, to control the narrative.

As she rounds the corner onto the narrow sidewalk of Nile

Corniche, the same woman she'd glimpsed earlier materializes from the shadow of a palm tree. This time, she stops square on the pavement. A challenge tied to Noura's very blood. Then the woman's attention flicks to Theo, who is bustling to catch up. The woman tenses before she spins, lifting the edge of her scarf to hide her face as she flees.

Noura chases in a horrific sprint. Her lungs, ravaged with too many emotions, reject the air.

The woman dashes between cars. Lights catch her face for the barest of moments. Despite the shadow floating across her, Noura is sure now.

Estelle is in Egypt.

Grab your copy today:
https://beautifuluglyme.com/my-writing/the-scorpion-thief/ OR
https://amzn.to/4pdVBbG

RECIPES

If you're curious about the desserts mentioned and have a hankering to taste them, here are a few recipes to try.

♀

Egyptian Quince Cake
  Ingredients

- 2–3 medium quinces (about 1 lb / 450 g), peeled, cored, and diced
- 1 cup (200 g) sugar, divided
- 2 Tbsp lemon juice
- 2 cups (250 g) all-purpose flour
- 2 tsp baking powder
- ½ tsp baking soda
- ½ tsp ground cinnamon
- ¼ tsp ground cardamom (optional)
- ½ tsp salt
- ½ cup (115 g) unsalted butter, softened
- 2 large eggs
- 1 tsp vanilla extract

- ½ cup (120 ml) milk or laban (fermented milk/yogurt drink, common in Egypt)

For serving (optional)

- Custard sauce, whipped cream, or thick Greek-style yogurt with honey

Instructions

Poach the quinces

1. In a small pot, combine diced quince, ½ cup sugar, lemon juice, and just enough water to cover.
   1. Simmer for 15–20 minutes until the fruit is tender but not mushy. Drain and cool.

Prepare the cake batter

1. Preheat oven to 350°F (175°C). Grease and flour a 9-inch round cake pan.
2. In a large bowl, whisk flour, baking powder, baking soda, cinnamon, cardamom, and salt.
3. In another large bowl, cream butter with remaining ½ cup sugar until light and fluffy.
4. Beat in eggs one at a time, then add vanilla.
5. Mix in the dry ingredients alternately with milk/laban, beginning and ending with flour.
6. Gently fold in the cooled poached quince.
7. Spoon batter into prepared pan and smooth the top.
8. Bake 35–45 minutes until golden brown and a toothpick inserted in the center comes out clean.
9. Cool 10 minutes in the pan, then turn out onto a wire rack.

Serve

Traditionally, Irish apple cake is paired with custard—at Groppi's, it might have been offered with crème anglaise, or in Egypt you could pair it with thick yogurt and honey.

♀

Irish Apple Cake
Ingredients

- 3 medium apples (Granny Smith or other tart baking apple), peeled, cored, and diced
- 2 cups (250 g) all-purpose flour
- 2 tsp baking powder
- ½ tsp baking soda
- ½ tsp ground cinnamon
- ¼ tsp ground nutmeg
- ½ tsp salt
- ½ cup (115 g) unsalted butter, softened
- 1 cup (200 g) sugar
- 2 large eggs
- 1 tsp vanilla extract
- ½ cup (120 ml) milk or buttermilk

For serving (optional)

- Warm custard sauce, cream, or whipped cream

♀

Instructions

1. Preheat oven to 350°F (175°C). Grease and flour a 9-inch round cake pan.
2. Prepare dry mix: In a medium bowl, whisk flour, baking powder, baking soda, cinnamon, nutmeg, and salt.

3. Cream butter & sugar: In a large bowl, beat butter and sugar until pale and fluffy. Add eggs one at a time, beating well after each, then stir in vanilla.
4. Combine: Add flour mixture in thirds, alternating with milk, mixing just until combined.
5. Add apples: Gently fold in the diced apples.
6. Bake: Spread batter in prepared pan. Bake 40–45 minutes until golden brown and a toothpick inserted in the center comes out clean. Cool 10 minutes before removing from pan.
7. Serve: Traditionally this is served with pouring custard—the silky sauce is what makes it distinctly Irish.

ABOUT THE AUTHOR

Janyre Tromp is an award-winning, best-selling historical suspense novelist who writes fiery myth-laced tales that, at their core, hunt for beauty—even when it isn't pretty.

Her books include *The Scorpion Thief, Darkness Calls the Tiger,* and *Shadows in the Mind's Eye.* But she's also a mom, award-winning editor, and wrangler of all things—including her fantastic teens and crazy fur babies.

You can find her on her website, www.JanyreTromp.com or social media (@JanyreTromp).